STRINGBEAN
AND THE
GRACE OF DOG

GENEVA ZANE

STRINGBEAN AND THE GRACE OF DOG

GENEVA ZANE

PINK
NARCISSUS
PRESS

This book is a work of fiction. All the characters and events portrayed in this book are fictitious or are used fictiously, and any resemblance to real people or events is purely coincidental.

STRINGBEAN AND THE GRACE OF DOG
© 2019 Geneva Zane

Cover illustration & design by Siolo Thompson

Published by Pink Narcissus Press
Massachusetts, USA
pinknarc.com

ISBN: 978-1-939056-16-0
First trade paperback edition: July 2019

For my father,
with all the love Dog gave me.

PART ONE

STRINGBEAN AND THE END OF THE WORLD

Who hasn't heard the story of how Stringbean was born?

So it is so: Father Christoph planted a patch of dirt with a tendril of Phaseolus vulgaris, and he prayed and prayed to the Almighty Dog for the earth to grow in choking fronds, something for the meek to chew on. And the King of Our World must have been listening, for the next morning, there, chubby hands wrapped in soft green feelers, was baby Stringbean, brown as the day was long. Tiny miracle. But this cannot be what really happened, though little Stringbean, who grows like a weed every day, too tall for her t-shirt and slacks, tells everyone: "I came from a pod!" And so, says Father Christoph, it was so.

Who hasn't heard the stories of Stringbean's life? The time it seemed Stringbean would never learn to walk, but the instant Widow Jahopson looked away the little bean ran on pudgy baby legs clear into the neighboring territory, and Father Christoph had to borrow the butcher's delivery van to track her down in time for supper. Or the time Stringbean turned all the church's windows upside down, and nobody was sure how she did it. Horrible, uncontrollable Stringbean! Where did she come from?

"Her parents are Cannibals," comes the bleached whisper in supermarkets and sitting rooms, over bubbling vats of liquid carbon in the plasticine factory. "Her father is her uncle," hiss lipstick stains on coffee cups, tiny nods and knowing smiles, yes, "She was dropped, and vaccinated, and got too much sun."

"I came from a pod," shrieks Stringbean, gallant and reckless on her bicycle, no hands. Look how her hair is pushed back from her face, how her eyes glimmer with danger, squinting in the dry sunlight. Others, hapless companions, cannot keep up with her pace or her stories, but of course they're all true.

The time Bubba and Stringbean switched the letters on the town sign to mean nothing at all, the time Stringbean filled a washing machine at the laundromat with dirt and grew a whole carpet of watercress before someone got her, the time Rose was lost for three days but Stringbean never told.

"My little Peapod," sighs Father Christoph, "Why are you so bad?"

"I'm just the way Dog made me, Father," she whines, upside down on the sofa, smartass since the day she bloomed.

Tall, lanky Stringbean, barefoot and freckled, something quiet behind the loud smile. Chubby, baby-fat String-bean, black with dirt and leaving footprints in the rectory. Poor little Stringbean, where did you come from?

"From a pod," she tells herself in a whisper, knees scraped and bicycle wheel still spinning.

From a little seed, and so it was so.

STRINGBEAN AND BUBBA

Little Stringbean, sun-browned as the Earth, was lonesome for nothing. She had Father Christoph, who hummed while he cooked, and Widow Jahopson, who sang when she was alone, and her own bicycle, once red but now rusted a colorless brown. She liked best to be outside, gobbling sunlight like the old days, never wearing a hat or protective goggles. She also had Dog, and what else, says Father Christoph, could a little girl need? She did not have playmates outside of the congregation, and even those kept their distance, for while they sang in sweet voices exalting their Lord and all things He had made, they were afraid of the earthy miracle that emanated from Stringbean's very skin. She did not care, and scorned their devout attempts to meet the immaculate bean by the river, by the railroad tracks. Stringbean did not long for the company of others: they were too slow, and they did not follow her orders without question. Except, of course, for Bubba.

John "Bubba" Vetch could not have been more adrift from that dirty miracle on the outskirts of town. His mother, like all mothers, worked at the plasticine factory, making fake flowers, which draped wildly on every surface of his home. "You don't even have to water them!" she'd exclaim with exaltation over her handiwork, though the time she spent dusting their stiff petals was surely longer than it would have taken to tend a garden. He was not allowed to ride a bicycle without a helmet, go outside without goggles and gloves, or have animals of any kind. His father, a laborer in the mines, was never home, and when he was he smelled repulsively of uranium.

Worse still, Bubba had no love of Dog, and scorned Father Christoph's flock from beneath his bike helmet and goggles.

She learned all this from the heady declarations of the church, who loved to revile as much as they loved to pray. "That boy may look nice," Widow Jahopson whispered to Stringbean as they greeted the Wednesday congregation at the church doors, "but he's got a mean streak inside him bigger than the tail of a rocket ship."

"How big is my mean streak?" Stringbean asked, looking at the strange, goggled figure in the distance. She wondered if he was hot beneath his plasticine weave poncho, and if he looked like a snail without a shell beneath it, writhing and cracked open.

Widow Jahopson laughed, a rarity, and it seemed to catch on the radiated sunlight like a leaf in a stream. "Little Peapod, there's no good in you to begin with!"

Stringbean could only agree, and held no bitterness towards this assertion. In fact, she felt only a warm and curious affinity with the mean boy across the street, wobbling on his bicycle but never fully falling.

★★★

When church finally ended, and Father Christoph wished them all strength and fortitude, to go with the Grace of beloved Dog, ("Beloved Dog!" the congregation echoed) Stringbean slipped outside, ignoring her usual duty of picking up crumpled pamphlets and left behind change. The boy was still there, almost perfectly round beneath his layers of clothing, even though the sun was heavy and huge overhead. Stringbean felt stuffy and hot even looking at him, and she wondered if he would come swimming with her, in the muddy brown river which snaked along the edge of town, where the congregation sometimes went to pray and throw stones.

Stringbean could feel Bubba Vetch observing her, even from his impious distance, and she allowed herself to be taken apart. Everyone she met looked up and down with a critical eye, trying to find the invisible joinery which was the irrefutable mark of Dog, the answer to a baby whose parents were dirt and divine. And what did they see? That she was tall and lanky, like grass that needs to be cut. That her rust colored hair did not lay flat upon her head, but rose in crow-like spines and feathers. That she wore only a tank top and shorts and no shoes, practically bare to the dangers of burns and tumors and dissolution—so opposed to trai-torous Bubba, safe from (and secretly terrified of) sun poisoning. Perhaps another would assume that these were two boys, met at the top of the River Hill to exchange natural treasures, one from the alike suburbia, and one from the backwards church of Dog, had it not been for Stringbean's weak chin, the noble declaration of girl.

Whatever Bubba had thought, she had no way of knowing, but she knew he did not like what he saw.

"Do you believe in Dog?" he asked suddenly, tightening his grip on his bike handles.

Stringbean beamed. "Yes!" she said, glad that the boy was done staring at her and now she could show him her bike, not as glisteningly beautiful as his, but better because it was hers.

To her surprise, the boy glowered. "I don't," he said, twisting the handles of his bike so the front wheel dug a trench in the red dirt. "Dog is dumb."

Stringbean could hardly speak. Dog was an unquestioned presence in her life, something she had been sure of since she was barely a sprout. What else could explain that almost physical lump of love she could feel lodge itself in her chest whenever she saw Father Christoph at the pulpit, or Widow Jahopson brushing her long, thin, ocean-brown hair, or her bicycle, or the birds that sang in the morning while she brushed her teeth? How else could you explain the wind, or the river, or the uranium mines, or how buildings stayed up? How could you explain Stringbean herself, born from a patch of dirt because Father Christoph had prayed and prayed?

Without hesitation, Stringbean reached out and slapped Bubba across the face. It made a good, loud noise, and she knew instinctively that it would bruise in the shape of her hand. "I'm going to get my bicycle," she told his watery eyes and pained round mouth. "I'm going to get my bicycle, and then we're going swimming in the river. And I don't want to hear anything like that again or I'll tie you to the railroad tracks til the sun's cooked you right through, and then eat you up like a bug." She glared at him with all the meanness Dog had given her, and then turned away, walking leisurely to the shed where her bike was kept.

Perhaps, watching the crooked annunciation cross the earth she was made from, Bubba Vetch, small, silent tears drifting over his swelling face, felt a little lump in his chest, like a flower blooming, like a bruise forming. Perhaps he tried to look upwards, to see the tall spire of the church, but his vision was clouded by his sun goggles.

And maybe, with a shaking, sweaty hand, he pushed them up his face, and, for the first time in his life, saw the sky stretching above him, bright, hyacinth blue and crackling with the grace of Dog.

(PAUSE)

"Dear Dog," Father Christoph murmured, one hand locked with the Widow's, the other with Stringbean's. "Bless this meal you have given us. Bless these roots, torn from your earth; bless these leaves, ripped from your roots, bless this fruit, plucked from your leaves. Keep us well, our Dog; keep us warm and fed and able. Have Grace."

Oh Dog, Stringbean thought, while Father Christoph and the Widow began to ladle food onto her plate; *if you know who broke my blue cup, strike them down.*

STRINGBEAN AND THE ERRAND

Little Stringbean, do you have a plan for today? "Of course," she answers, scowling the way only Stringbean can, "but I'm not telling." What are you doing today, little Peapod? "Something," she answers, arms folded across faded green polo shirt. "None of your business."

"Stringbean!" Father Christoph called from the garden, catching her as she tried to creep away from the rectory. "Will you run an errand for me today?"

"Why should I?" Stringbean grumbled, but she trotted over to him all the same. Her feet crunched in the dry grass, the same color as the cicada husk she had displayed on her windowsill, a glassy, translucent brown.

"I need you to mail a letter for me today. Do you know what a letter is, Stringbean?" His voice was not unkind, but his face had the open, sympathetic expression that she hated, for Stringbean hated to be looked at, body of Dog that she was.

"No," Stringbean answered shortly, picking at the dry skin around her thumbnail.

"Do you know where the post office is?"

Stringbean scrunched her slight face in concentration. "Next to the library?" she guessed.

Father Christoph nodded happily and tousled her hair. "That's it, Peapod. Do you think you can do this for me?"

"I guess," Stringbean answered, moody. She did not like having her hair tousled, or being touched by anyone, even Father Christoph who had prayed for her to be. Of course, that did not matter to wild, obstinate Stringbean, who would have found a way to sprout even without him.

"The letter's in the kitchen, next to the door. And Stringbean?" he called as she began to slink back to the rectory. "Ask Widow Jahopson if she needs anything."

The letter was where he had said it would be, a thin white rectangle marked with jointed writing that Stringbean could not read. She took a perverse pleasure in how the clean surface of the envelope became smudged by her dirty hands when she snatched it from the counter. She took a moment to admire the dark red stamp in the corner, and another to try and decipher the Father's writing, but it was no use, and with a lopsided shrug she padded into the living room in search of Widow Jahopson.

At first the small, dim room seemed empty, and Stringbean squinted at the furniture, not quite ready to think about where else the Widow could be. But then the room adjusted to Stringbean's eyes, and the Widow appeared like a vision before sleep. She was sitting in her usual place by the front window, in her rocking chair. Her long, dark brown hair was undone and hung in waves over her blue dress. Widow Jahopson's clothes never seemed to fade the way Stringbean's did and the blue was just as vibrant and electric as it had ever been. Stringbean's shirt had a hole in it, an amoeba-shaped rip near the hem; she bunched the fabric in a fist, so the Widow would not see and sigh, a sound that seemed to push all the air out of the room as well as her lungs.

Her head snapped away from the window at the sound of Stringbean's heavy footfalls, and she regarded the tattered little girl with eyes that seemed not to see at all.

"Father Christoph wants to know if you need anything," Stringbean asked in a whisper, standing at the arm of the rocking chair. The Widow looked back confused, her beautiful, tanned brow crumbling, and Stringbean rushed to clarify. "From the store. Do you need anything from town?"

The Widow's eyes were unfocused, drifting from the front yard to the frayed couch to Stringbean, poor little Stringbean hesitant in her torn shirt and dirty shorts. A waif-like hand rose to the Widow's glowing skin, so slow that it looked for a moment as if somebody else, some specter, was caressing her cheek with light, bored touches. Stringbean shivered, and was ashamed, and longed to put that hand in her own, to fill it with blood.

"Nothing," the Widow said to the plywood radio. "We need nothing."

And she was torn back into her reverie. Stringbean did not think to ask if the Widow was mistaken, that the rectory was in fact crying out for stamps or nails or olive oil. She did not ask if the tab had been settled at the general store, and if she should bring some change from the jar they kept on the window sill. Stringbean needed to be free of the hot, inside air: the letter was already a sticky ball in her fist.

★★★

Something big inside her rejoiced at the feel of the dirt road beneath her feet. It was more than just the tactile pleasure she gleaned from being outside, working in the garden, swimming in the river. No, it was the pleasure of having somewhere to go, and being able to go there on her own. Stringbean moved with agency, as she always did, but it was her own kind of agency, and she went as fast as she wanted. She stopped to pretend: she was a soldier, she was a cowboy, she was an astronaut. She squatted at the side of the road and shouted encouragement at the patchy grass, urging it to grow big and strong like her, Stringbean. She vaulted over the barren potholes that scarred the road, raising her little arms in victory with each successful crossing. She was jubilant, and alive, and unconnected to the stuffy exchange she and the Widow had shared. She didn't think about that. She was good at forgetting things.

The sun didn't waver; it never did. Stringbean had not once in her short life spent a day without the embrace of sunlight: even on the rare days of rain, the sun shined bright and clear. Father Christoph had sermonized on the subject a few times, and the congregation had risen and cheered and collapsed like a heartbeat, but Stringbean, relegated to a back pew where she could look out the window and pick at her scabs, felt no connection to them. She did not pray for rain. She prayed for bubblegum, fireworks, and a spaceship. The sun did not waver. It barely sank, heavy as a sponge, when Stringbean finally reached the outskirts of town.

It was a town fit for Stringbean, scrappy and one minded, though Stringbean had never belonged within the suburban arcs of Prominence. She was most comfortable in the stretches of forest that bled into the outskirts, for the town existed in and out of nature. It lay in a valley of mountains that looked purple when the sun set, clutching the river to its chest in uneasy intimacy. The relationship was a passion. The river ebbed, receding so far that it was now just a listless brown stream. The town shifted its boundaries, redrew lines for reasons that Father Christoph and the radio grumbled about at dinner, but Stringbean never listened. The plasticine factory up on the ridge rumbled, and spat, and kept everyone going. The mines were invisible, but they were everywhere, like veins under skin.

Bubba lived in a house somewhere along this road, one of the houses that were distinct from each other but made identical by their nearness, their sheer number. Stringbean did not want to be with him today. She liked to be solitary, sometimes; she liked the independence of having a plan for the day, a destination and intention to be exacted with her own kind of meticulousness. Stringbean did not have patience for inefficiency. She did not have patience for much of anything, except what she and Dog had decided was worth doing, and who knew the mind of Dog better than she did, she who had been cast from his most wicked thoughts?

The errand itself did not particularly bother her—she was upset that her plans, so careful and painstaking, had been averted, but she enjoyed the straightforward nature of this adventure, a goal so direct she could feel it growing sweaty in her hands. The dirt road had become a smattering of asphalt slabs, tapering off down the main street. Stringbean's eyes roved the line of buildings with distaste. Their order, their regularity, their distance from the earth made her bristle with uneasiness. There was the youth center, and the general store owned by a member of the congregation and the town hall and the laundromat and the miner's union building and factory-shuttle stop, and there, the little white building beside the library, was the post office. How quickly, Stringbean mused, errands seem to end when you are thinking of other things.

**

It must have been shift change. There were men wandering the streets with lunch pails and aimless destinations (the factory had only one shift, so no women could be seen). They impressed Stringbean greatly, with their dirty faces and their effortless power, each step the step of someone who had worked, and worked hard. She straightened her back and tried to walk like they did, her soft chin tilted arrogantly, her skinny arms pushed deep into the pockets of her shorts. But she could not affect the heaviness they carried in their thick work boots, nor could she emulate the expression of savage pride on their faces. She could not keep her mouth composed, not with the burning scent of uranium heavy on every body she passed.

They did not call to Stringbean, though some of them knew her from church, and others knew her from trouble she had caused and drew their hoods accordingly. They did not ask where she came from, though she would have delighted in telling them of her miracle. That was a discussion for weekends, when laughter did not bring the dust of the mines with it, or after work, with their wives, who knew the details more definitely than this strange, grubby child. The truth was speculative and fluid and unanimously agreed upon. They could not waste their hour in the sun on her.

Stringbean, though she never counted her sunlit hours, felt a similar apprehension at the door of the post office. She did not want to leave the warm day, to reenter the stuffiness of indoor weather so soon after she had escaped it. Her eyes would swim, her breath would come short, her feet would feel gritty on the tiles, and that was a sensation she hated above all others.

The work bell rang, clanging and lively, but it could not disguise that its call was that of a funeral. Everyone in the square, all the men and one little girl, took a last deep breath, and plunged into their caverns, where the light of Dog could not touch them.

But the post office was not humid, like she had expected. It was cool, and made Stringbean's lungs feel as if they were full of moisture, like she had somehow swallowed a cloud. She had seen a certain type of cloud in one of Bubba's picture books, white and frothy, like something that would taste sweet, not at all like the clouds that hung listless as cantaloupe skins above the chapel. The post office reminded her of a picture book cloud—clean, but cold. Its white tile floor and its blue counters and the tiny metal postboxes that lined the walls were all gleaming with efficiency. The postboxes appealed to Stringbean immensely. She liked their numbered windows and their glistening dials. She liked anything she could keep secrets in.

"Can I help you?" someone asked with the characteristic annoyance which curled in the voice of anyone who had the displeasure of talking to Stringbean. They could tell, she knew, that she was a miraculous creature, and they were envious, as all who do not pray are envious of other's miracles. Otherwise it was a good voice, Stringbean conceded, strong and direct, like the Postmistress herself.

"I gotta mail a letter," Stringbean answered, crossing her arms and her eyes and letting her canine teeth show. She couldn't fully see the Postmistress, not over the tall blue counter, but she could see a high forehead and thin eyebrows, and she didn't like them.

"You *have got to* mail a letter," the Postmistress corrected. She was tapping her pen on the counter and it ground against the cool air.

Stringbean scowled her meanest scowl. "I don't *have* to do anything." Her words were sharp as briars, the kind that scared Bubba and saddened Father Christoph, the voice of someone who chased cats and killed birds and was mean because Dog had willed it to be.

Somebody behind the counter laughed and said something Stringbean could not hear. The Postmistress replied with a huff, though she did not sound angry. In fact, when she spoke to Stringbean again the annoyance had cleared from her voice, and she leaned over the counter so her square, strong face could be seen.

It was a good face, Stringbean decided, all together.

"Where's that letter headed?" the Postmistress asked. Her eyes were ice-blue, her button-up frock a startling white, the kind of clean Stringbean's hand-me-down t-shirts could never dream of being.

"I don't know. I can't read the writing." She did not clarify that she could not read at all, had never been taught and had never wanted to learn.

The Postmistress extended a large hand, and String-bean, on tiptoes, placed the crumpled envelope in her palm. For a moment, the older woman's brow furrowed in consternation, unhooking Father Christoph's scrawl, and then, once she had decoded it, furrowed deeper. The bright eyes that had so impressed Stringbean now looked at her with an uncomfortably open expression. It made String-bean feel suddenly naked, and she took a reflexive step away from the counter and stared at her feet.

She doesn't have to look at me that way, Stringbean thought with a sudden fury. *I'm just the way Dog made me.*

The Postmistress was talking to the other person behind the counter, a hushed conversation that Stringbean was too enraged to follow. She could almost taste her anger —if, when she had entered the post office, she thought she had swallowed a cloud from a picture book, now her throat was full of the hot, dry smog that hung above the plasticine factory. How dare these women pity her, she who had more than they ever would: her own bicycle, her own room, a porch where she could sit in the evenings and make up songs. She wished she still had the envelope, so she could crumple it, tear it into tiny pieces, and throw those pieces into this woman's face…

"Do you want to put your letter in the mail chute, honey?" the Postmistress asked, interrupting Stringbean's fantasy. Her expression was controlled again, her voice direct and knowing, the endearment that punctuated the question more like fact than affection. It cut through Stringbean's hazy rage, which cleared into a curious emptiness. She didn't want to be angry. She wanted something she wasn't sure of, something physical and embarrassing, and to give this unknown longing a known direction, she nodded quietly.

The Postmistress led Stringbean behind the counter, which had a similar icy cleanliness as the main room. A tall, dark haired woman, the source of the laughter, sat at a cluttered desk sorting letters and packages into various containers, wisps of hair floating in an airy halo around her head. She smiled and waved at Stringbean with her fingers, but Stringbean was too confused to wave back.

"Right in here," the Postmistress said, gesturing to three slots on the far wall, each with a word above them. Stringbean noticed she did not say 'honey' this time, and it made her stomach ache.

"The bottom one," the woman at the desk called, and the Postmistress handed Stringbean the letter, which had been ironed out, and seemed to shine with the same perfection as when Stringbean had found it on the kitchen counter. How long ago that was, she thought; and no time at all. She realized she did not want to put the envelope through the mail slot, though the Postmistress was watching her expectantly, and Stringbean would die if she disappointed her. What would happen next? What had been her plan for the day? She did not want to swim, or play pretend, or search the riverbed for turtle eggs. To leave the post office would be torture, but there was no escaping it.

She pushed the letter through the gap, feeling it drop down the shoot, feeling her stomach drop with it. Where was it going? Where would she go now? Stringbean felt the loss immediately, and wished she could get the letter back, wished she had been quick enough to shoot her hand inside the slot and catch it before it fell. Stringbean thought she heard it land, soft and solid.

Stringbean pretended she had never let it go.

"There," said the Postmistress, with a vague pride. "All done."

(PAUSE)

Bubba Vetch had lots of friends, more than he could count on both hands, and all had their advantages. Lenny had a bike with ten speeds, which his father had bought for him almost six towns over. David's mother made army guys in the plasticine factory, and so his room was overrun by olive-green soldiers, forever paused mid-combat. Kid had a slingshot. Jake had an allowance. Tim was allowed to eat candy. Ike had seen the ocean. When Bubba entered the gentle ova of their playrooms he tallied these merits instinctively, and ranked his affections accordingly.

But none of them had what Stringbean had: a knowledge of what could be taken, and a fire to take at all costs. She knew where the animals slept in the forest, and she was not afraid of their fangs. She was dangerous, fearless, and insatiable. So Bubba found himself in the churchyard most days, heart beating hot and face uncovered.

"Where are we going?" he'd ask when she finally emerged from her chores, pants rolled up to her knees.

"Wherever I want," his hero answered, teeth bright in the sun, and Bubba knew he wouldn't trade her for anyone in the world.

STRINGBEAN AND THE RIVER

Little Stringbean, baked dry as a terracotta urn, trudged barefoot through the center of town, her breath the thick heaving of a dissenter fleeing the rages of war. From far away she heard the church bells echoing and cringed with guilt, but the hot air propelled her quest, even if her heart pounded and her stomach was in knots.

Bubba, in contrast, couldn't have been happier. He had convinced his best friend, the brave and disreputable Stringbean, to skip her Sunday service and go down to the river with him. To swim! On a day as hot as the desert, the sun burning mean red brands on skin that dared to approach. He was not bothered by the heat, his sun goggles and hood stashed away beneath Stringbean's bed, his sleeves rolled up and his dark hair pushed back from his face. How cool it felt, free of his layers! Oh, what a day!

This must be what Dog feels like, he thought joyously, flexing his fingers in the warm air. He still had his sneakers on, stained brown by dry red dirt—he couldn't comprehend how Stringbean could be barefoot her whole life. Didn't it hurt? And didn't she fear the mysterious mercuries of the Earth? He shook off thoughts of disease—that didn't matter anymore, for he was brave, and strong, and could keep up with Stringbean without tiring.

"Remember when we switched all the letters around?" he asked Stringbean as they passed the town sign: *"Welcome to Prominence, Home of the Uranium Battery!"* (rearranged: *mcoWt eHme ttniu oclnomoman ! inPthef yrrB ee,eo nUrae*). It had not occurred to him that Stringbean's declaration did not have an occult significance, for he would never have guessed that Stringbean could not read, that he possessed a power which she did not.

Stringbean only nodded; she was not interested in her previous exploits, only future ones. Her heart still wrenched when she thought about the service she was missing and the punishment she would receive when Father Christoph found out, when he inevitably read her mind later this evening, but her worries were dispelled when she pictured the river, murky and cool, listless in the embrace of the shore. And, even though it twisted her stomach, it was a pleasure to escape the dense heat of chapel, Father Christoph declaring hope and peace to a chorus of cheers, the furtive glances to where Stringbean was, and today, where she wasn't.

The two fugitives veered from the road into the patchy forest by a thin, winding path, branches reaching out to stroke their arms and catch in their hair. Stringbean ignored Bubba's little whimpers of pain when his soft skin was pricked, ignored the loud tramping of his sneakers in the underbrush. She moved easily, unimpeded, a creature of Dog at home in His vast kingdom. The woods, their cluttered underbrush and nest of branches, were where Stringbean ought to be on a Sunday morning, not in the chapel, half-asleep. Where was Dog anyway, if not in the woods, in the croaking of birds and the bone-white moss?

"Are you sure this is the right way?" Bubba whined. He did not feel as good as he had when they were taking the main road, and the sky had been clear and huge over his head. He'd been cut by a thorn bush, and his allergies were beginning to act up, so every couple steps he had to pause and wipe his eyes with his shirt. Worse, he could feel the hum of a sunburn buzzing across his neck, whispering cancer with each twinge of pain.

"This is a shortcut," Stringbean lied. Once they were out of the forest, they still had to climb down the gulch and follow the train tracks until they found a part of the sea wall that had collapsed. Stringbean preferred this circuitous route to the main road: she liked to jump the fallen logs, to scramble beneath overgrown bracken. But she didn't want Bubba to go home yet, which he would certainly do if he learned that what they were doing was not what was easiest. Despite his whining, his slowness, his lack of grace or athleticism, Stringbean wanted to have him with her. It calmed her heart, made her reckless and bold, just as she was supposed to be.

***

Bubba fell down a sand patch in the gulch, and String-bean burned her foot on the metal rails of the train tracks, but they kept cheerful, daring each other to leap from high places, exchanging jokes and stories. Of these, Bubba's were heavily fabricated, and grew more fantastic as the sun got higher in the sky, but it was impossible to tell if the adventures Stringbean related (the time she had thrown a wad of chewing gum into the post office mail slot, the time she'd hiked to the next town over and found that it looked exactly the same) were true or not. Bubba, his mouth open and his eyes wide, accepted each word from his hero's mouth to be as sure as fact, and nothing could shake him from this belief.

So when Stringbean finally turned off the sea wall and down to the rocky riverbed, Bubba Vetch was in consider-ably better spirits. The river, it was true, was never as good as what he could imagine; not at all like the poster in his mother's room (white sand, blue water, "Get away from it all!" emblazoned in soft pink letters against a clear sky). Instead, it sat, a strange, erased line across a landscape of skeletal trees. The sky seemed dim beside the river, as if its color was being held beneath the surface, clutched in the sucking hold of the swirling silt. The bed was made of sharp black rocks, broken from larger pieces by the tattered waves, and again Bubba was thankful he had his sneakers on.

"When I was eight I swam from one side to the other," Stringbean bragged, shucking off her shorts, "and it wasn't as low back then." The river had ebbed as the drought deepened, until it was so narrow Stringbean could almost skip a stone all the way across it, for some other her to find. Yet, even in this crude form, the river had a heaviness, the awe-inspiring power that is possessed only by Dog and His Earth, and Stringbean longed to conquer it.

"That's impossible," Bubba said, carefully removing his shoes and pants, so the cuffs were not stained by the gritty shore. "There's a big trench in the middle. It'd suck you right under."

Stringbean narrowed her eyes. "That's not true."

"Sure it is," Bubba said, bringing his folded stack of clothes far away from the waterline. "It's science. Peter told me."

Peter! Peter was slippery and pockmarked and one time he had taken Stringbean's bicycle without asking. Peter still held his mother's hand when he crossed the street. Peter hissed at Stringbean when he was with Bubba, but quaked before her when he was alone. What did Peter know that she, Stringbean, did not? Without bothering to answer Bubba, Stringbean strode forcefully into the water, its limpid coolness immediately bringing air back into her lungs.

"Stringbean!" Bubba called from the shore, his knees

bent and only his feet in the water. She was beginning to regret not leaving him back at the main road. "Don't go out too far!"

The water did not part easily for her thin body, and she felt as if she were pushing it aside with each labored step. Her beater and underwear clung to her, heavy and damp, but finally free of the sweaty stickiness she'd held since that morning, panting awake with the blankets pushed off her pallet and the wooden floorboards swollen. Her room was always the hottest in the rectory, since it was the highest up and had only one window, which, on hot nights, stuck shut, and besides, let bugs in. But everywhere was hot on a day like this: the kitchen had been unbearable, and even the shade felt slick and oppressive.

"Stringbean!" Bubba called, but his voice was quieter now, and Stringbean ignored it.

The water was only up to her chest. She was not worried for the moment when she would no longer be able to stand: she was a strong swimmer, just like she was strong at all other things. Father Christoph had taught her to swim back when she was still small and pudgy, his hands on her sides while she learned to kick in time with the curl of her arms. She'd nearly shot out of his arms when she'd found her rhythm, or so he liked to say. Stringbean liked to swim the way she moved: loud—huge, exaggerated kicks and strokes that would splash anybody nearby.

"Stringbean!"

Now, when they went to the river, Father Christoph preferred to float upon the surface while Stringbean paddled around, and the Widow, when she could be persuaded to accompany them, never got in the water. Stringbean could not understand why—the pleasure of the river was perfect and whole. The mud beneath her feet felt pleasantly soft, like the silk scarf the Widow had hidden in the back of her chest of drawers. How cool and easy everything was in the river! She let her hand trail through the tides behind her, enjoying the weightlessness of her body, the freedom of her movements. She was almost halfway to the other shore. Bubba didn't know anything.

"*STRINGBE—!*"

The last syllable echoed frantic through the water, and she was swallowed up.

★★★

The earth had disappeared, as sudden as a door slamming, and pulled little Stringbean down with a choke of surprise. She struggled to see, flailing wildly, but she seemed to not move at all, and if her eyes did not burn with each passing second, she would have thought they were closed. The water was so heavy, and so dark. She was sinking, sinking.

I've been eaten, Stringbean thought hysterically, *by a whale.* And what a delightful thought it was, for a moment, to allow herself to sink deeper into the maw of the inevitable, no escape, and no use in trying. What was little Stringbean to the king of beasts, the terrible Leviathan, now that she was locked in his stomach far beneath the sun? There was nothing left to do but dissolve, and dissolve she shall.

But no—here was no place for hysteria, not now, and Stringbean pushed her terror down into the deep. With a furious effort, disjointed and inelegant, she kicked her legs, propelling herself through the silty water, shoveling it aside like she was digging a tunnel. Her lungs were beginning to burn, stabbing in her chest, tightening, wrapping around her throat. The river was a tomb of stone, crushing her bones and stealing her air. What had happened to the hot day? What had happened to the relief she had felt, seconds ago, when she had waded carelessly into the chasm? Stringbean felt her muscles would snap, the cold was so sharp and pounding. She could not see the surface, or any sign that she was swimming in the right direction. She couldn't see anything.

"Oh, Dog!" she screamed, but her mouth filled with water, heavy and viscous as lead. Her limbs were iron. Her head felt full of air, light, drifting. With each push forward, she felt her body drag further down. What was her prayer going to be, after that? Had she planned out anything besides her initial shout; was her last pocket of air doomed to be spent on a hollow admission?

Oh Dog, forcing her limbs upwards, crawling with no air inside her. *Oh Dog, Oh Dog, Oh Dog.* But she could get no further.

What do I have to say? she thought to herself, raising her aching arms for one more stroke. *There has to be something to say.* She wished she had said something to Father Christoph before she left this morning. She wished she could see Widow Jahopson, sitting at her vanity, her faint hand resting on a string of pearls.

With a tearing noise, her head broke the surface.

***

Bubba cried loudly and miserably the whole way home, holding onto Stringbean's waist like she'd slip into the earth again. The moment of Stringbean's disappearance had been the worst of his life, as he stood helplessly on the shore, running forward and then pulling back again. Even when Stringbean had finally surfaced and dragged herself to land, he could not control his hysterics.

"Bubba," she had shouted, her voice husky and weak. "Bubba, I need your help." But all Bubba had wanted was to run away, to leave her broken on the shore so that he would never have to feel such pain again.

"Oh, Dog," Stringbean murmured into his shoulder, stumbling along the forest path.

He gritted his teeth and helped her walk, clasping tight when she stumbled. Her body seemed smaller now that he was supporting it, holding her steady through the tangled forest path, her skin cold white beneath her freckles, her chest barely moving with each shallow breath.

"Oh, Dog," she coughed, her body shaking against Bubba's. "Oh, Dog."

How much longer until he could get help? How much longer until this torture was done? Why had he, Bubba, been chosen as witness to this tragedy, he who had never hurt anyone and never would?

There is no Dog, Bubba thought angrily, hot tears sliding down his sunburnt face. *There is no Dog.*

(PAUSE)

The radio, a monstrous thing, was turned on during dinner, and turned off long after the Father carried String-bean up to bed. It squawked and hummed and sometimes had to be hit so the static would clear, but the noise it made was part of its personality, and Stringbean almost thought of the radio as a fourth guest at their dinner table, coughing as it related the news of the world.

"Officials of the North-West territories reported promising statistics on the mercury levels of local water sources today…"

"Ah!" Father Christoph scoffed. "What is promising? Promising for us? Promising for them? Promising for Dog and the promised land?"

Stringbean did not listen; she chewed her food loudly and waited for eight o'clock, when the dishes would be cleared away and the news would end and the radio would buzz with stories of pirates and cowboys and outer space…

STRINGBEAN INTO SPACE

Little Stringbean, skinny as a weed, lay on her back with her arms splayed out beside her, the rusted frame of her bicycle a dull blur in the corner of her eye. The sun pulsed like a fan-blade, and Stringbean was languid and happy in its brilliance, illuminating her dark skin, tight over lean bones. Her mind groped lazily for the words Father Christoph had read to her about Dog and the sun, but they floated half-formed over her eyes—there was no need for such things in her sun-drenched canopy, her storm in the eye of Dog.

Her hideaway was a small, private solace: a wide dirt clearing in a tangle of dried up trees. Stringbean and her bicycle could steal away here, for precious small moments between lunch and supper, when she tired of Bubba and swimming and the buzz of Father Christoph's radio, reporting static disaster after disaster while he shook his head and made notes for Sunday's service. Her fingers burrowed idly into the earth, and she felt a raucous, pounding joy at the gritty feeling beneath her fingernails.

She thought, with uncommitted curiosity, of the dirt she had come from, the patch in the Father's garden from which she had been plucked. Nobody else she knew (though, admittedly, it was a small number) had grown from a seed in the ground—but this did not cause String-bean any distress. The powers of Dog, as Father Christoph liked to say, were beyond reason and like no others. String-bean liked the sound of that: "like no others." In that sense, she and Dog were the same.

Her thoughts wandered, floating freely in the peaceful air. Why did the moon change shape? How long until her birthday? What would be for dinner tonight? She thought about the news report she had heard at dinner last night, about a spaceship sent to the Crab Nebula, piloted by a man whose name she could not remember. It had excited Stringbean greatly—it was just like a comic book, or a radio show! But the Widow had frowned, and Father Christoph had shaken his head, though he could not speak with his mouth full of potato shoots, and by the time he had finished chewing a new story had come on about the caverns and the raid that was being organized.

"What are they looking for?" he had asked Stringbean and Widow Jahopson with feigned wonder. "Treasure? Water? The underground cities of Dog's first people?" He'd snorted at his own joke and Widow Jahopson had smiled beatifically, chewing her food with a delicate resolve.

Stringbean, her eyes barely visible over the ledge of the table, had pushed her potatoes and peas together, the fork like a hammer in her hand.

"The only thing in the caverns is radiation," she remembered Bubba telling her once, his tone dark. "And cannibals." They had been hunting birds and Stringbean had hit one, but they never found where it landed.

"And treasure," Stringbean had added, tossing a stone into the air so it became a little speck in the blue, blue sky.

The idea of treasure made Stringbean shiver with excitement. She could picture herself, a brave archeologist like the man on the radio, plundering the depths of the underground for sparkling jewels, their splendor surpassing even the string of freshwater pearls that Widow Jahopson had in a little velvet box at the back of her dresser. *For the people of the future,* the man on the radio had said. Stringbean pictured herself returning, weary and beaten by radiation, bloodied by her battles with the cannibals, a relic of ages past (an emerald, a machine gun, a toy sailboat) clutched to her chest. *For the people of the future,* she would say with somnolent wisdom, raising her treasure so it could be seen by her crowd, before passing it off to the little case of memorabilia on display in the town hall.

Or, Stringbean thought wickedly to herself, she would find a stronghold of riches deep in the cannibal dens, the hollow cities, and return to Prominence a tyrant, more powerful than even Ms. Regen, owner of the uranium mines. Yes, that would suit her better than a silly card in a cabinet which she wouldn't even be able to read. Imperial Doge Stringbean, she who collects the tithes!

But better still, she thought—rolling over to recapture the circle of sun, which had listed dramatically in the passing of time—she would capture the ultimate treasure: the real location of Dog. Yes, it would be Stringbean, suited in her carbon-weave spacesuit and pale green space ship, who would charge outside of Earth to find the answer to everything. That would show the congregation, who scoffed at her perfect miracle, and would not let her play with their soft throated children. Sustainable life! That had been the phrase the spaceman had used, though she did not know what that meant.

She imagined that was what Dog was: life, and a word she didn't know.

Did Dog come from a seed? Stringbean thought to herself, her neck crawling with the grit of earth. She would ask him when she found him, somewhere in the crevices in space. She would ask him who his first people were, where their city went, how buildings stayed up, when her birthday was, why she was so mean, why Widow Jahopson would stare out into the garden and sigh heavy as an atom bomb...

There was a shattering, rumbling, screaming noise, so loud that Stringbean's ears buzzed, eyes shook in her skull. A cacophony of animals sparked in the underbrush, everything rushing for escape. The skeletal birds who had been roosting in the bald trees took off all at once, their broad wings lurid in the dead air, calling in panic: Are we safe? Are we all here? They wheeled and dodged and screamed, so loud and tangled that Stringbean could hardly think, could barely breathe.

Something terrible had happened, that much was clear. Stringbean lifted her bicycle and dragged it through the brambles, not even bothering to watch where her feet landed. All around her, animals cried for each other, wailing and howling, then falling silent. Thorns caught in her heels, and her blood was lost in the red dust of the road.

Then the air was deathly quiet, except for the crack--crack of her bicycle wheels and her heavy puffs of breath.

***

The spire of the church leaned high above the tree line, and Stringbean exhaled a clutched breath in relief that it was still standing. She could hear the whine of an emergency, now that she was closer to the town, and began to run, pushing the dead weight of her bicycle away, moving so graceless and heavy that her lungs began to heave before she was even halfway there.

"Father Christoph!" she screamed, forcing the heavy door of the church open, and immediately she was swept up in the Widow's arms, pressed close to her chest. The Widow was crying: silent, beautiful tears that seemed to complete the picture of tragedy that she carried always. Stringbean reached up with a calloused hand and pushed one away, leaving a streak of dirt on the Widow's perfect face. Behind the Widow, as if from an immense distance, she could hear Father Christoph praying and the telephone ringing, and again, the siren, but in the embrace of the Widow, she felt a safety and joy like she had never known.

"Come on, Peapod," the Widow whispered to Stringbean. "We must pray now."

"What's happened?" Stringbean allowed her bleeding feet to be led where Father Christoph knelt before the altar. He seemed like a fixture of the chapel, as immovable as the pulpit and the pews, the faded stained glass windows and the crack in the tiles Stringbean had made when she'd dropped the stone angel she'd been trying to steal.

"An explosion at the Uranium mines," Widow Jahopson said brokenly, sinking to her knees beside the Father. "We must pray for Dog to have mercy on their souls."

Stringbean clambered awkwardly beside them, clasping her hands and bowing her head. The uranium mines were a maze of tunnels, white-cloaked miners, silent as nuns, gently scraping the walls for ore. An explosion could collapse the entire mine, like Stringbean and Bubba crushing anthills with their bike tires. *Buried alive,* Stringbean thought with a sting of dread. Sinking in the dark while the air slowly disappeared, or maybe just crushed, dying instantly. Which would be worse? She thought of Bubba's father, and the two men who lived above the library, and the whole family in the dock house by the river, and anyone else who could be trapped by the mines right now. Her mouth moved, following the lead of the devoted beside her, but her thoughts wandered to a corner of the Crab Nebula, where Dog looked down on her world.

Oh Dog, she asked silently; but she could think of nothing more to say.

(PAUSE)

Oh Stringbean. If only you had been born in a time of music, a time before the earth broke open and all the melodies escaped into the sky. If only the body of sound beneath your skin could be wrapped in the valves of a trumpet, the hammers of a piano. Hum for us, Stringbean, while you work in the garden, while you sit in the pews, any tune you can imagine, because they are all new now. Is that your voice, rising strong and clear above the congregation? Is that you, walking to the river with a song in your teeth? Oh, Stringbean! the things drums could be in your hands!

STRINGBEAN AND THE SEED

Little Stringbean, warm and heavy as a stone, ripped tattered weeds from Father Christoph's vegetable garden, freeing bounties of tomatoes and cabbage from choking bonds. The tearing noise of strands from dry earth delighted her almost as much as the feeling of sweat on her neck. Father Christoph, his slacks stained and his heels digging small trenches between the rows of glowing produce, sat on the edge of the plot, breathing heavily, puffing little prayers for the creatures we must kill to keep the meek alive.

Stringbean liked the garden. She liked the feel of dirt padded flat by her bare feet, her work boots growing mossy with dew under the porch. She liked the soft itchiness of vegetable fronds reaching out to brush her freckled shoulders as she moved through each row, slow and methodical. She liked the sting on her palms, wrapping the tendrils of weeds around her fist and pulling the roots free.

"Stringbean?" Father Christoph called from the edges, his voice muffled by the plant walls Stringbean idled in. Her first instinct was to ignore him, to stay warm and tired in her seclusion, but after a moment she trotted to his summons dutifully, though she did not step from the boundaries of the garden.

"I have something for you," he said with a wise smile that folded his wrinkled face so severely that his eyes could not be seen. Stringbean's breath stuttered with excitement. She never longed for objects, not seriously—in fact, she had everything she could ever want—but she loved little affections: a can of soda from Widow Jahopson (smuggled away from the moralizing gaze of Father Christoph), an especially smooth stone from Bubba. She kept them in a line on her windowsill, where they caught the light of the moon and made strange shadows across her bedroom wall.

"What is it? What'd you get me?" she demanded, trying to uncurl his concealing fist, but he just laughed and held it high against the backdrop of the sun.

"Patience, little Peapod," he chided. There was an undercurrent of gravity in the statement, though his face remained cheerful. Stringbean watched expectantly as he leaned forward.

With the slow, precise drama of a fruit unpeeling, the Father opened his hand to reveal a little seed, sitting whole and perfect on the fat of his palm. It was black, and round, and like a drop of water, the seed fell from Father Christoph's calloused hands into Stringbean's small, smudged ones.

"What will it grow?" Stringbean breathed, cupping the beautiful thing delicately in her fingers. It weighed nothing, of course, but she felt the same heaviness she felt in church and when she couldn't sleep at night.

"That is an apple seed," Father Christoph said, wiping his hand on his slacks, though there was no dirt to be seen. "If you water it, and keep it warm, and pray to Dog every day, it will grow into a strong apple tree."

She nodded, her thoughts skipping and scratching like the radio did. Her own tree! Not one of the skeletal firs that stretched desert hands into the sky, surrounding the church in a ragged half circle; no, a strong, alive tree with curling branches and bright red fruits, round as rubber balls. She could not remember the taste of apples exactly, but the word sounded full and clear in her mouth, like a swallow of fresh air, bursting from the silt surface of the river for a sweet, clean breath.

"Do you want to plant it now?" Father Christoph asked kindly, his old hands resting on his knees, his smile easy and adoring, no hint of the hardness from earlier. Stringbean could only nod her head, too engrossed in the little life she held in her hands. She followed the Father blindly to a corner of the yard, where, she saw, he had already torn up the grass and turned the soil. Small lumps of earth rose in a line, where Stringbean guessed Father Christoph had already planted other trees, other fruits.

"Dig a little hole," he said, kneeling down to the spot he meant, and she complied readily, happy to feel the dirt between her fingers. "Now place the seed in. Make sure it's facing up… that's it. And now cover it, all the way and a little more."

"This is how I was born," Stringbean said, happily distracted. Just the same way Father Christoph had planted a seed that grew her, she was planting a seed that would create a tree taller than all the others around. She wondered what *her* seed had looked like: smooth and round like the apple seed, or flat and white like a pumpkin? Had it had fallen as easily into the earth, or had it resisted a little, sticking to the Father's calloused palm before sinking into the ground?

"Yes, indeed it was." Father Christoph answered with a little laugh. "Now, do you promise to come out here and water it every day, and pray to Dog every night, so your tree may grow?"

"I promise!" Stringbean said, jumping up from the dirt wild and erratic, like a toy that had been flung. She wanted to express her gratitude, but she hated to touch, to hug. The Father did not seem to mind her distance, and stood creakily, humming a song Stringbean knew but did not recognize. He carefully brushed the dirt from his clothes before pushing in the screen door, and disappeared into the rectory. Stringbean stayed outside, her toes splayed in the grass, listening to the bugs hum and waiting for her seed to grow.

***

Stringbean watered the seed every morning, and prayed to Dog all the prayers she could remember, even if they didn't have anything to do with growth. The days grew too hot to wait outside in, and too long to watch for signs of growing. She and Bubba would spit off the Chapel balcony, but the droplets of saliva would be gone before they hit the loose earth. She would lean far over the railing, her feet off the ground, watching the little white orb disappear in a sizzle of air, while Bubba stood with his jaw clenched, back pressed against the window.

"What if you fall?" he hissed, his hands tight fists around the frame. Stringbean fixed him a mean look, and leaned further, practically upside down, while he screamed and begged her to come down.

At last she acquiesced, and they clambered back into the chapel. They were supposed to go swimming, and Bubba was impatient to leave before the sun got low, but Stringbean had to water her seed. He huffed impatiently, wrapping his towel in his hands like the cord of leash.

"It's just a dumb apple," he told her, while she dragged her watering can from the porch faucet to the patch of dirt her seed slept beneath. "You can buy one at the store."

"Shut up," she told him, her arms shaking with the weight of the water. "These apples will be *my* apples." She didn't want to tell Bubba that she had never been to the grocery store. It was too far away even to bike to and Father Christoph didn't have a car. Besides, they grew all their own food, except what they were given by members of the congregation, or bought from other gardens and barns.

"I wanna go swimming," Bubba whined. "I hate fruit."

Stringbean wanted to hit him, but she didn't want to miss a chance to go swimming, and he always went home when she got mad. "Listen," she explained, trying to keep her voice level. "This is going to grow into the biggest tree ever. And I saw it when it was a little seed. It was this big, Bubba," she said, holding her hands so only a sliver of space remained between them, "and it's going to grow taller than the church!" She pulled her arms back to their full extent, her face breaking into an uncontrollable smile.

And maybe, something dark inside her whispered, *it'll grow into a person like me.*

Bubba frowned, then fiddled with his goggles. "Food from the dirt makes you sick."

Stringbean gave up trying to explain. Bubba never got anything anymore. He never took off his hood or his shoes, and he never ate any food from the rectory. She couldn't even remember what his face looked like, except it was clean and almost pink in its whiteness. There was no way he could understand the importance of seeds, and what it was she was doing when she poured water on the ground, when she whispered little prayers into the dirt. "I thought you'd stopped wearing your goggles," she challenged, standing straight so she was a little taller than him. His face flushed, and she smiled to herself, opening and closing a grubby fist.

"I am," he swore. "I just... forgot to take them off today."

"Take them off then."

"I'm going to! Just... in a minute."

Stringbean decided she was tired of fighting with him. She could win whenever she wanted, even if he was almost her height now and threatening to get bigger. "Come on. Let's go to the creek. It's gonna get dark soon."

***

At night, tucked into her ragged pallet, Stringbean thought secret little hopes. Maybe, instead of an apple tree, a person just like her would grow from that beautiful seed. The person would not be like Bubba, who could never keep up with her, and never understood what mattered; nor like Father Christoph, who was always telling her to pray; nor the Widow, who looked at her with such tragic, perfect eyes. They would not be like the man who ran the laundromat, nor the woman at the town hall, nor all the other people who came from other people and not the grace of Dog. Moonlight landed in hard rectangles around her, and she smiled to herself, imagining the companion who would grow. Yes, the seed person would be just like Stringbean: dirty and mean and unafraid like Stringbean, tall and fast and strong like Stringbean.

She thought of names for the seed person, but never dared to say them out loud, because she knew Dog might hear them as the wrong kind of prayer.

Each day Stringbean watered her seed, and each night she dreamed of the adventures she and it would share. They would swim, of course, and climb trees, and ride bikes, and Stringbean would show it her secret hideaway, which nobody but her knew of. Where once the days had been long and hot, now evening began to fall on the rectory like a wave hitting the shore, a rhythm that grew quicker and quicker with each passing week, as if a storm was forming just off the coast, just out of sight.

One day, after the sun had begun to set, Father Christoph came out to where Stringbean was crouched by her seed. She had been watching for life, like she did every evening now that the days were getting shorter and cooler, and was not thrilled at his company. She couldn't think of the adventures she and her seed would have with him there, because he could see when she was thinking bad thoughts. Stringbean tried to clear her mind, reciting all the prayers she could remember, as, with a creaking of limbs, he knelt down beside her. His expression was stony, and Stringbean felt a spiral of guilt start in her stomach, and began to pray with a new fervor, not meeting his eyes.

"Have you been watering it?" he asked Stringbean, looking at her, but not seeing her, as if she were an animal he had struck down. She nodded—her whole body felt choked, as if she was being squeezed by some unseen hand, the air lurching from her lungs until there was none left. "And have you been praying to Dog for an apple tree to grow?" She nodded again, more adamantly, but her eyes were wide and wet with the truth.

Father Christoph sighed heavily, then rested his head in his hands. "Oh, Stringbean," he murmured, "What have you done?"

She could not answer, ashamed of all she had asked for, even if it hadn't been aloud. Had Dog heard? Had he listened to every fantasy, growing more and more disgusted? And how could she think this wouldn't happen? What claim did someone like Stringbean have to a miracle? "I..." she said haltingly, hearing the lie in her voice and flinching from it. "I prayed..."

"Why are you like this, little Peapod?" Father Christoph lamented, not really asking, resting a delicate hand on the spot where her seed had once been. His white fingers looked, for a moment, like bones, like a skeleton draped across the dirt. "You know we do not ask for what we don't deserve. You know we don't pervert Dog's creation."

"I didn't mean to. I didn't… I'm just the way Dog made me," Stringbean stuttered, curling her body so she couldn't see the little patch of death she had created, the little grave for the seed she'd killed. "I'm just the way I am."

Father Christoph sighed harder, placing a hand on the back of her neck. Stringbean felt like she should be crying, but she couldn't—all she had was a horrible ache in her stomach, heavy and cold as wet earth, filling her throat and burying her alive. *I killed her,* she thought to herself, but who even was she? Blurred, Stringbean tried to remember who this imagined friend had been, but she could not draw the particulars, only the broad necessities: she was strong, and brave, and her name was a treasure greater than any Stringbean owned.

"We do not make as Dog does. We do not stain what He has given us with creations from our wretched forms," Father Christoph said. The sun was setting, but there was still a faint light, a tinge of pink in the air around them. Soon it would be dark, and Stringbean would lie in bed, watching the shadows change and thinking of a friend she never had. "We are too easily mistaken. It is only Dog who makes no mistakes."

Then why, Stringbean thought, as the garden sank into darkness, *did Dog make me?*

(PAUSE)

Stringbean spat on her hands, and wiped the dust on her shirt. A streak of dirt stretched across the pale green fabric, but Stringbean did not care. She did not pay much attention to her clothes; anything was fine, as long as it did not restrict her movements, and her shirt collars did not choke her and her shorts had deep pockets. Sometimes the holes these latter articles accrued in accidents and adventures would be converted into still more pockets by Widow Jahopson and her thick, copper needles.

Purely, and without question, Stringbean did not wear shoes. "It's because she's a child of Dog!" Father Christoph would cry, delighted, when he saw her striding up the dirt road, no hesitation in her step. The soles of her feet were three or four shades darker than the rest of her body, and hardened like coal. She could walk across the rocky beach of the river without altering her step. She could jump from the top of the stairs to the bottom without making a sound.

STRINGBEAN AND THE FLOWERS

Little Stringbean, dirty and smudged, waited on Bubba Vetch's doorstep, feeling mean and alive. Bubba was at his peewee football game, a bleak concession of his mother on the condition that he always wear his sun goggles whenever he was outdoors. And while Bubba had argued and fought and thrown his cleats at the window (where they bounced harmlessly against the 900% protective plasticine surface), Stringbean knew he was relieved that he would no longer have to risk the damage of the sun.

She sighed, watching the road for the Vetch's pea-green station wagon to turn with infuriating slowness into the driveway. Her long, spindly legs stretched out in front of her, and, pleased with herself, she observed their dusty brown color, so different from Mrs. Vetch's almost blue-white translucence. This was Stringbean's chief meanness —she made sure her sun-sodden skin was vibrantly displayed whenever she visited the Vetch's home, and the pleasure she felt at Mrs. Vetch's obvious disgust was second only to the new-found pride of riding a bike holding only one of her handlebars, and when Widow Jahopson sang while she brushed her hair.

Stringbean did not often visit Bubba's house, as she

was not allowed inside, and, in all honesty, had no interest in being invited. But Bubba had not been by the rectory in some time, and though his weakness annoyed Stringbean, she had many plots that required two people, and Bubba was the person to do them with. Beyond that, she had been feeling listless and bored, and maybe, deep down, a little lonely.

Humming a song she had just made up, Stringbean reached down to the front lawn, hoping to find some dirt she could rub on her hands and possibly stain Mrs. Vetch's impeccable white skirt, only to jerk her fist back in shock. The grass, instead of yielding pliable and soft to her rooting fingers, had been rigid and sharp, refusing to bend, even to quiver. Another tentative exploration confirmed: the grass, the whole lawn, was plastic. Each individual blade had been stuck into the earth with a diabolical uniformity, maliciously green and rich, outshining the neighbors' yellow-green lawns with a palatable smugness.

Rage like she had never known filled Stringbean. Mrs. Vetch, with her squinting eyes and high, nervous voice, had never been an enemy: only a victim. But now, as Stringbean sat so hot and furious she couldn't even move, she saw that Mrs. Vetch was the evil Father Christoph warned about, the trembling renunciations of avarice, edifice, decadence. A plastic lawn! When Dog had created every blade of grass Himself and Stringbean herself had been born from the earth!

With this thought, Stringbean at last roused herself to action. She leapt from the stairs and wrenched at the door-knob, tugging fruitlessly against the locked catch. Of course —Mrs. Vetch would never leave her home unguarded from any danger, be it the stained hands of an intruder or the sizzling beams of the sun. Undeterred, Stringbean circled the house, her bare feet stabbed by fake grass with every frenzied step, but the windows were all locked, and she knew they were unbreakable. But she expected no less from her enemy; Stringbean's victory would be all the more celebrated with the breaching of this fortress, like finally cracking open a peach stone to see the white threads inside.

At last, her torn feet padding with agony on searing asphalt, she arrived at the garage door, which hung as shut and final as the seal of an envelope. Stringbean stood in a moment of pause, readying herself, then wrapped the door's handle in her calloused fingers. Skinny arms trembling, she lifted the door six inches before the lock caught and refused to budge. But it was enough. Sucking in her stomach and turning her head, Stringbean thrust her body under the barrier and into enemy lines.

***

The first thing she noticed was the smell. The rectory where she lived smelled like many things: wet wood, lilies from funerals, Father Christoph's vegetable garden, Widow Jahopson's perfume (when she wore it, on special occasions, it lingered for days), and the unidentifiable smell of the sun that drifted through wide windows. "It is people who fear Dog that fear sunlight," Father Christoph would always remark gruffly when he saw Bubba's goggles and hood. It was a scent Stringbean wanted to carry with her, that she hoped her skin emanated, sun warm and brown.

The Vetch house smelled like nothing. Not even the stale, dull taste of air that the church smelled like on Sunday mornings before anyone arrived; not even the lingering smell of gasoline that clung to other garages like skin.

For a moment Stringbean stood, her anger abated by a quiet, shaking unease. She crept across the garage towards the door, a pace and volume she was not used to. Stringbean, when she moved, was brash and athletic, never subtle or quiet. "You're making a racket, Stringbean," Widow

Jahopson would moan on her days of headaches, when she couldn't bear to eat, or even stand up, and Father Christoph and Stringbean had to make raw vegetables so as not to bother her with the smell. Stringbean, with the choking affection she felt only for Widow Jahopson, Father Christoph, her bike, and Dog (and sometimes Bubba when he wasn't crying or fidgeting with his shoelaces), would try her hardest to be silent and unseen, yet her feet always betrayed her.

But now, in the total silence of the Vetch House, Stringbean moved as gently and imperceptibly as a planet. The door fell open without a sound, and the pure white expanse of the kitchen, the sitting room, and the dining room appeared, impassive, before her eyes.

Everything pulsed with a vicious cleanliness. The counters were devoid of seeds or crumbs, the floor was free of dirt, the lampshades and the blades of the ceiling fan were barren of dust, and Stringbean, usually so unapologetic, even vindictive, in her dirtiness, felt for a moment a shiver of powerful shame. She did not belong here, that much was obvious from the beginning; but there was something greater, harsher, in the perfection before her, as if her very being was an offense to the house's existence.

On every surface, the only surges of color among the white furnishings, like blood on the tundra, were hundreds of plastic flowers. They lounged full and heady in vases, were draped with precise carelessness in wide bowls, swaddled lifelessly in heavy bouquets, or stood tall and proud as a solitary focal piece on each table. Their colors were blinding: heart reds, desert yellows, blues so blue Stringbean's mouth burned with the taste of lightning. These were the trophies of Mrs. Vetch's hours in the plasticine factory, carving clay molds with a delicate nail file, her pale eyes only blinking every couple minutes, her hands never shaking.

Still sneaking, still moving without sound, Stringbean crept across the alive clean space until her dark feet reached the foot of the stairs, her hand tightening on the spotless banister. It was strong and synthetic beneath her hands, as if, when the water finally drained away from the Earth and the world collapsed in on itself, the banister would remain, a snaking path to a higher place that no longer existed. The rectory's stairs to her attic room were made from unpainted plywood, and shook if anyone larger than herself dared to ascend.

The walls were hung with photos of Bubba: Bubba at school, Bubba at his birthday party, Bubba in his bedroom, a red plastic car clutched in his fist and a scowl on his face. Stringbean paused before each of them, her brow crushed in confusion. She had seen photographs before, pictures of fields, animals, or new babies that members of the congregation pushed before Father Christoph, and though the Father refused to touch their chemical surfaces, he smiled and beckoned Stringbean to look with him. But she had never seen a photo of someone she knew well, and she studied the photo of Bubba's football team with exaggerated care. There was Kid, with his slack, lopsided face; and Peter, whose eyes were squinted; and Bubba, who looked like Bubba, but not at all like the little boy she had shared adventures with since she was a child. There were no pictures of the family, or if there were, Stringbean was not interested enough to look for them.

The upstairs was as clean as the floor below, the sparse, white hallway dividing into four doors. Stringbean stood before the first one, shaking slightly. The doorknob, glistening silver like the treasures Stringbean dreamed of, was the bright antithesis to her dirt-smudged hands, and for a moment she could not bear to tarnish it. But she was brave, and strong, and forcing her arms upwards, she took the knob in both hands and tugged.

It was locked. Stringbean did not bother to force it, though she burned with curiosity at the secrets that Mrs. Vetch could keep.

The second door led to the bathroom, which sparkled white and spotless, and did not interest Stringbean in the least. The cabinets, she was sure, were filled with the same things as hers at home: toothpaste, shaving cream, and supplements in paper packages, for the Widow's headaches and the Father's indigestion. The next door, however, was much more interesting. Bubba's room was filled with toys, scattered across the floor and shoved in labeled containers. Posters hung on the walls, depicting sports teams and mountains and soldiers with guns, and half the room was dominated by a bunk bed that Stringbean stared at longingly. Kneeling on the floorboards, Stringbean took a dark green truck into her hand, pushing it across the ground and making soft noises of speed. A strange elation filled her as she pushed the truck faster and faster, before letting it go, laughing as it shot across the floor and flipped against a yellow convertible.

The last was Mrs. Vetch's room, unremarkable save for one plastic lily on the bedside table, and the floating smell of uranium her husband must carry with him everywhere.

★★★

When she had entered the Vetch home, her mind had been consumed with the slight Mrs. Vetch's disgusting falsities had cast at her, but now, standing in the center of her enemy's soul, Stringbean's mind began to tick with revenge.

Her first instinct was to rub her face, her hands, on the immaculate white sofa and armchair, long streaks of dirt like roads in the snow. But Stringbean knew, when she moved into the plastic silence of the living room, that a part of Mrs. Vetch would enjoy the act of cleaning, that she thirsted for it, longed for cosmetic disruption, which could only highlight the perfection of the rest of her home. No, that would not do. Stringbean's revenge had to be lasting, irreversible, a raised red scar on Mrs. Vetch's pale stomach.

Distractedly, Stringbean traced the petal of a plastic chrysanthemum, its purple tongues unfolding with mathematical precision. How long had Mrs. Vetch slaved for this one imitation, bent over a mold in the plasticine factory, breathing shallowly behind her surgical mask, mixing the hot vats of plastic until she got the color she wanted? And the other women, the ones who produced the little cars and action figures that littered Bubba's room, which gleamed with similar exactitude; how long did they spend, carving little miniatures in a churning factory where no sun could reach? Stringbean had never considered what it was that the women she saw walking to the smoking towers, bright plastic lunch boxes clutched in their gloved hands, were really doing, but now, her dirty fingers clutching this fake flower, she understood something she couldn't name, something impossibly and futilely sad.

Quietly, she said a prayer to Dog.

Then she began.

Taking flowers into her arms, Stringbean carried cluttered bouquets into the kitchen, stuffing every delicate mimicry into the Vetch's state-of-the-art gas oven. When it was full, she set the oven to six hundred degrees, standing on a chair to reach the buttons, and began to stack the remaining flowers directly onto the ranges, turning each to their highest setting. The smell of melted plastic began to fill the house, bright colors popping and searing with a desperate hiss. Stringbean watched in fascination, the determined fronds and pistils becoming water before her, mixing into a poisonous green-brown and dripping over the sides, onto the white tile floor.

Such destruction! Dog-like, Stringbean marveled. Her previous exploits, her pranks and trespasses, seemed childish in this moment. Meanness bubbled inside her, as lazily as the bubbling plastic ooze, and she suddenly felt dizzy, and clutched the back of the chair for balance.

So entranced was Stringbean with her evil she did not hear the garage door open with an electric hum, and the car rolling inside and sighing to a stop, nor did she hear the door to the kitchen being pushed outward, the clack of immaculate heels and the clatter of cleats.

She heard a scream, like that of a train.

She felt a hand on her shoulder, jerking her away from the oven and pushing her against the counter, her body twisted at a painful angle, long, oval nails digging deep into the back of her neck.

"You little slut!" Mrs. Vetch screamed, her long face red as an animal. Out of the corner of her eye, Stringbean could see Bubba, sweaty from his football game, standing dumb and trembling in the door to the kitchen.

"You unspeakable cannibal!" The hand that was not constricting around Stringbean's shoulder collided with her face, and she felt her teeth shake. "You unwanted pagan! This is my house! You fucking monster! You filthy cunt! I'll have you killed! I'll have you strung up and thrown in the caverns! Do you think you can do this to me? Do you think you can come into my house and destroy my beautiful things, you goddamn devil? Do you think anybody cares if you die?" With every pause for breath her free hand struck Stringbean across the face, a sharp smack that sounded like a gun. Stringbean was crying. She saw that Mrs. Vetch was too, huge, heavy tears. Stringbean's face burned. Her eye was swollen shut. She could taste blood.

"Bastard," Mrs. Vetch sobbed over and over. "You bastard bitch." Her blows were weaker, as if her hand was too heavy to lift. The smell of plastic was everywhere. Stringbean could hear the colors popping on the stove, could feel molten plastic dripping onto her neck. "Your mother should have drowned you. You should have been killed by that lunatic priest."

Stringbean fell into the pain, into the words spit from that snarled lipstick mouth. Each curse seemed to complete an image she didn't even know was fragmented. It was if Stringbean had been finding the scraps of some great document her whole life, and now the complete work was being shouted at her, and she did not have the strength to cover her ears. She could see, at last, what she looked like in summation: what all the pieces had not been able to show her. Mrs. Vetch's words clicked into her, though she didn't know what they meant; she just knew they were true. She was all of those things. She felt her body go limp.

Oh Dog, she thought through a bloody mind. *Oh Dog, oh Dog, oh Dog.*

PART TWO

STRINGBEAN AND THE ROSE

There goes Stringbean, flying by on her bicycle. Her shirt whips around her middle, her sandy hair pushed back from her gaunt face, spokes rattling, teeth rattling. What joy! She stands balanced on the pedals, like a conqueror hooked in the stirrups of a warhorse: charge! Imperator Stringbean, general of the sun, flying so fast the earth blurs. With a shout of laughter, she throws up her arms, holding the wind in her spread fingers, holding the world together with her bravery, her power, her grace.

There goes Stringbean, bucked from her bicycle with a mighty crack, like lightning striking a battleship and tearing it in half. Disgraced, Stringbean skids, her arms searing with grit, her eyes squeezed shut, the feeling of soaring still gentle on her brown skin. Oh hubris. Does no one escape?

She landed in a bony heap, and there she stayed, taking silent stock of what limbs remained. Her fingers? They moved, curling, unfurling, with careful slowness. Her arms? She could feel the tears on her elbows, interrupting the freckled pattern with a crater of sticky red. Her pride? Battered, but, she rationalized, piecing herself together on the asphalt, at least no one saw.

But then Stringbean heard a sweet chord of laughter from the top of the hill. Shading her eyes, she saw a figure gliding easily down the steep incline, no fear in her step. Even from far away, Stringbean could see ink-black hair and a sharp jaw, relaxed with laughter that bubbled from sweet lips as if it could not be held back. She felt a flutter of panic. It had been years since she had talked to a person her age, and much longer since she'd spoken to a girl.

"That was quite a fall," the stranger (for she was certainly a stranger) said when she finally arrived, kneeling down to where Stringbean lay in a crumpled heap. "You shouldn't have let go of the handlebars like that, it upset your balance."

Stringbean cringed, thinking of Bubba Vetch's friends, their bicycles glinting like money in the sunshine, coasting easily through the town center, arms crossed behind their covered heads. "I've done it before," she replied, surly with embarrassment. She wished, suddenly, that her gray t-shirt did not have holes in it, that her clothes were as immaculate as the girl before her.

The stranger nodded solemnly, and Stringbean saw that her eyes were black as her hair, black as a serpent, little specks of white along the edges of her pupil. Her skin was white too, not the sick whiteness of the women in town, no, a pure, strong white, like marble. For a moment, Stringbean felt the same way she had on her bicycle: victorious and powerful, as if the world was suddenly in reach and waiting to be hers.

Remembering her fallen steed, Stringbean turned her battered head to where it lay, and felt the wind get knocked out of her a second time. The handlebars were bent almost at a right angle, the chain had become wrapped around the back wheel, and the frame, already rusted from its years of being hers, had a mighty crack running through the length of it, like a deep scar of battle.

"I don't think there's any fixing it," the other girl said, her voice factual, maybe a little cruel, as if she took great pleasure in delivering bad news.

Stringbean did not trust herself to speak. Her bike! Her greatest material object, her companion to all adventures, imaginary or not. To see it, lying impotently on the asphalt, made her throat tighten and her eyes sting, worse than the throbbing in her hands and knees. If she were not in the presence of this other person, Stringbean could have wailed for the loss.

"Maybe there's hope," the stranger said, perhaps noticing Stringbean's distress. "My dad's a physicist—he knows how to put things together. Do you want to take it over to him?"

"Don't worry about it," Stringbean mumbled, knowing she wouldn't be allowed in the girl's house anyway, not when her father saw how bad Stringbean was.

The girl pursed her lips, which reminded Stringbean of seashells. "It's no trouble," she said, rising to her feet and extending a hand to Stringbean. "I'm Rose. I just moved here."

Stringbean hesitated to take Rose's hand, worried she'd make it dirty, but after a moment she accepted the gesture, her long brown fingers almost completely covering the other girl's soft, white palm. It felt alive in Stringbean's grasp, like a bird or a drawing. "I'm Stringbean," she answered when she was standing, pleased to see she was a good three inches taller than Rose.

The easy peals of laughter Stringbean had heard from the hill bubbled up again. "That's your real name?" Rose cackled, her eyes little black slits, and Stringbean blushed. "Who named you that?"

Stringbean had never thought about it. It had always been obvious that she had been named for the seed she came from, but who decided that? "Who named you?" Stringbean countered, to avoid admitting her ignorance.

"My dad did," Rose answered immediately. "It was my

mom's name. Was Stringbean your mom's name?"

Again, Stringbean felt uncomfortable at the question. "I came from a seed," she answered, but it did not feel like truth the way it used to, under the scrutiny of this stranger, her eyes sharp and intelligent.

Rose nodded slowly. "I don't have a mom either."

***

The house Rose lived in looked like it was part of the surroundings, rising so naturally from the litter of scrap metal and abandoned possessions that it seemed to be one of them, a shack beneath the overpass that someone had broken and left behind. The outer walls were made of disparate planks and sheet metal, forming strange, cancerous-looking lumps where the wood had warped or the metal had buckled. The door had no lock, and it hung half open when Stringbean and Rose arrived. Stringbean looked to her companion, alarmed, but Rose did not seem concerned, only opened the door fully and entered before Stringbean.

The inside was the same disparate collection of materials. Cobbled from spare parts, it seemed to be a stitched together all-purpose room: on one side there were three cots, messily pushed against the wall; on the other was a make-shift kitchen. Dishes filled the sink and spilled onto the counters, the distorted floors. Everywhere there were cabinets and chests, overflowing with things Stringbean had no name for.

On the far side of the room was a door, which led, Rose told Stringbean, to her father's workroom. The wall between the two rooms shook whenever a car drove across the overpass, quaking so violently that it seemed it would take the whole house down with it. Gingerly, they placed the mangled bicycle beside the door to the workroom. "He's out with my brother right now," Rose explained, wiping her hands on her dress, "but when he comes back he'll fix it right up."

(Stringbean, taking in the collection of broken machines scattered around the bedroom, doubted this, but, in a rare moment of tact, didn't mention it.)

"Sit down," Rose ordered, pointing to one of the cots pushed against the wall. "I'll get some stuff to put on your scrapes." Before Stringbean could argue, Rose pushed her over to the mattress with both hands, then began to root through one of the many cupboards that hung, half open, around the small room.

Stringbean twitched nervously, watching the door from the corner of her eye. The mattress made her feel uncomfortable: it was too unstable, too suffocating, too difficult to escape if the time came. She made her body as small as possible, as if she would slip through someone's hands if they tried to grab her.

Stringbean was not the brash child who had so brazenly desired the world years earlier. She was older, and her demeanor was that of an animal that had been caught in a trap once before: one of her paws was a torn stump now, her teeth had tasted her own flesh, but she would never be caught again.

"Where do you live, Stringbean?" Rose asked, still upending the various containers around her room. She seemed to enjoy calling Stringbean by name.

"At the rectory," Stringbean answered, the words muffled by her never-still hands. "Outside the chapel on the outskirts of town. You can see the steeple from most anywhere."

Rose nodded, but Stringbean got the sense that she was thinking less about Stringbean's answer than the next question she was going to ask. "So you must follow Dog, if you live in the chapel?"

Stringbean bristled instinctively, but she did not sense

any animosity in the girl's question. "I don't live in the chapel, I live in the rectory. And yeah, I believe in Dog."

"Really."

"Yeah."

Rose's eyes flashed a little, and she looked Stringbean right in the face before asking her next question.

"And you believe Dog created all things?" she probed, not breaking eye contact. Stringbean's face flushed at the unabashed way Rose stared at her, but she did not look away.

"Yeah," Stringbean answered.

And now Rose's face flushed with victory. "If Dog created the world, and Dog is good, why is there evil in the world? Why would a being of pure good create evil? How does evil exist if there is a pure good that could destroy it?"

Stringbean, sensing that she had been led into a trap, said nothing. There seemed to be no way out of the verbal cage Rose had built, yet, strangely, it did not disturb Stringbean. She wondered if some part of her, without verbalizing it, had wondered the same question.

Rose, seeing that she was not getting a rise out of Stringbean, returned to her search, the vindictive glint her features had adopted falling back to the soft, petal-like face Stringbean had seen at the top of the hill, bright with laughter.

"Here we go!" Rose cried, emerging from a pile of odds and ends, a square, white case with a red cross on the front clutched in her arms. Stringbean smiled at her companion's excitement; it was curiously infectious. The scrapes on her arms and legs burned, and she could feel fragments of grit digging into her red skin. It was not unbearable—no worse than when Bubba and his friends had thrown her in the river, the heavy water biting her limbs and crushing the air out of her body, but she didn't think she should tell Rose that, after she had tried so hard to find the first aid kit. She didn't think she could tell Rose anything without choking.

Rose settled on her knees in front of Stringbean, assessing damage, taking Stringbean's head into her hand and turning it left, then right. Her face was very close to Stringbean's, and she was struck by how feminine Rose was, how each small detail (a sharp jaw, a full lip, a delicate, lidded pair of eyes) combined to create a figure that was undeniably female. Stringbean had a gaunt, sunken face, a combination of days spent outside and a diet of only vegetables. Her torso seemed too small for her body, so her arms and legs had the exaggerated quality of an insect, a similarity that was not aided by her slightly wide-set eyes.

Rose shifted so she was resting on her heels, and Stringbean saw the swell of breasts beneath her sundress. Stringbean had remained much the same way as when she was a child, muscle and bone, and she quickly spun her gaze away, ashamed.

"How'd you manage to get a black eye in a bike crash, Stringbean?" Rose asked, her voice a shade of the one she had adopted earlier, the voice that wove traps.

Stringbean reddened further. The black eye (and the trail of bruises arcing across her ribs) had been won in another fight with Bubba Vetch and his friends, all of whom had grown tall and brawny in the years of Stringbean's exclusion. Poor Stringbean had stopped growing last summer, a row of angry measurements on her bedroom wall cementing her failure with vivid, graphic obviousness. Rose looked like she had stopped growing too, but at the right height, the top of her head just level with Stringbean's nose. "I just did," she said shortly, looking anywhere but Rose's dark eyes.

"You're not mad at me for what I asked you, are you Stringbean? About Dog?" Rose frowned, and Stringbean's silence showed no sign of ending. "I'm sorry. My father asked me that question a few weeks ago, and I thought you could help me figure it out."

Stringbean suspected that this was not quite true, and she was resentful of it. "If you don't know, why don't you ask him?" she growled, trying to regain the advantage in this quiet battle she had unknowingly stumbled into.

But Rose did not seem to notice Stringbean's display. Her brow was furrowed, her eyes distracted. "He doesn't give me the answers. He only asks the questions. That's the whole point."

What the hell, Stringbean wondered, *does that mean?* Again she felt the walls of a trap rising, but she could not figure out its purpose, or, perhaps more importantly, whose trap it was.

But Stringbean was startled from her thoughts by a grip of pain snaking up her bones, emanating like sunlight from her skinned elbow. Gasping harshly, she jerked her arm away from Rose's grasp, shocked by the pulsing, wet hurt the girl had caused. Was this the trap, finally set? Her betrayal shined, unguarded, in her sharp features, but it did not perturb Rose, who laughed brightly, rocking on her heels.

"You're silly," she said, unfurling Stringbean's protected arm back into her hands. "The pain means it's working."

With able, focused calm, Rose moved from scrape to scrape, brushing each cut or bruise with a cotton swab and a frown of concentration that furrowed her brow. Stringbean wanted to reach out and push the wrinkles from Rose's forehead, but she felt paralyzed. Her arm did feel better, now that the stinging had subsided, and while Rose was not gentle, there was such determination in each caress of Stringbean's injuries she seemed to be willing the wounds to close, and Stringbean's body, perhaps feeling the same bewilderment as Stringbean, only complied.

The silence, once a defense against attack, was

becoming unbearable, a shield become a prison. She wanted to tell Rose something, but what? That she had never been so sure of Dog until this moment, but also, never more sure that she could live her whole life without Him? That she had no friends, no one to talk to, and that each halting word they shared made a flutter of panic shiver through her body? That she wouldn't even care if her bike never got fixed, that she felt she could move just as powerfully without it?

"I'm bad," she blurted out at last, to warn this sharp, direct creature who didn't seem to realize, to notice the wickedness that leaked from Stringbean's skin. But that wasn't what she'd wanted to say. "Big as a rocket ship," she amended, remembering something Widow Jahopson had said to her once.

"Oh, I know," Rose said, dabbing the maw of a wound without looking up. "But I'm even worse."

(PAUSE)

Stringbean's eyes were a bright hazel, a color too delicate for her tough face and thin mouth. There was a
strange, disconcerting quality to them, something subtly
wrong, but not in any obvious sense. They were eyes that
would have fit the Widow better, or Rose, but they were
Stringbean's, just like everything else.

There were secrets Stringbean kept to herself: dreams
she'd had, items she'd stolen, fights she'd lost. There were
secrets that were kept from Stringbean, and these grew
more frayed with each moment they were held. There were
secrets no one knew, not even the people who kept them,
secrets the universe whispered to itself. It knew that clean,
white stone buried in the mouth of the river, which no one
would ever live to find. It knew the left of Stringbean's wide
eyes was nearsighted, almost blind; a small aberration of
her body known by no one else. The universe folded
around Stringbean's strange eyes, a gentle layer of cotton
that had no weight, and no form, and nobody who looked
into Stringbean's face would ever see this; and neither, of
course, would Stringbean.

STRINGBEAN AND THE WIDOW

Humming thoughtlessly, Stringbean played with the hem of her shirt, fitting her fingers between the holes it had acquired from adventures and age. Her feet tapped against the porch steps, in time with whatever song she was creating, a song with no beat or rhythm besides what her nodding head decided. The air was humid, and carelessly Stringbean reached up and crushed a mosquito between her palms, a buzz of pride piercing through the haze of the day and lighting up her face. Stringbean also buzzed: her plans jolted and spun though her mind, while she tried with clumsy hands to pin them down. The beginnings of a day were rising like a tide, the agenda for her next free hours; but for now, the sun resting on her shoulders and the birds calling to one another, Stringbean was content to remain reclined on the rectory porch, tapping her feet and spinning thin, aimless thoughts.

Where would she go today? The river, maybe: she loved to swim, even while the river sank lower and lower, hardly even a stream anymore, and strange animals struggled to the shoreline for a mouthful of water. Their heavy, tattered forms made Stringbean feel cold, the broken irises of their slit eyes seemed to see everything she was, would ever be. They were not violent, and perhaps, if she was younger, Stringbean would have tried to fight one of them; even so, Rose, when she consented to travel with Stringbean to the black shoreline, viewed the animals with pity, and begged that they go home.

Or maybe she would make the trek to the post office, even with the sun like a gas fire overhead? She had nothing to mail, of course, and even if she had the ability to write a letter, there was no one she could send it to. But Stringbean enjoyed the cool sanctuary of the post office, and found excuses to visit it often: delivering letters for Father Christoph, or on rare occasion, Widow Jahopson. She liked to play with the knobs of the postboxes, and slip stamps into her pockets when no one was watching. She liked the busyness of the operation, the knowledge that while she did not know where the letters were going, someone did, and they would deliver them there without fail.

Or maybe she could take her bike and return to the quiet hush of her secret clearing, and watch the unchanging blue sky and huge, harsh sun…

From the corner of her eye, Stringbean noticed a shivering form, a wriggling smudge on the surface of the porch. Her fledgling plans were bashed to pieces almost instantly, and with the quiet clamber of a hunter, she crept closer, her face almost pressed flat against the steps.

The beetle's jaws were slight, like the crescent of a needle's point, but they pulverized the wood without straining, the runoff rising from the bite in pulpy waves. Its legs kicked, the last pair wriggling fitfully above the porch: the angle its curved stomach made left them unbalanced, not touching the wood, yet the sureness with which the beetle chewed had a particular strength to it, even if the rest of the body flailed and protested. Bending closer, Stringbean searched the black pill of its form for wings, but there were none, only a ridged armored plating and its smooth, blind head. Every breath she released shook its body slightly, and with a dull shock she saw small hooks curl from the delicate legs and grip the wood, never once stopping in its feast. Slowly, the porch's scratched paint and rotten surface were devoured particle by particle, as the beetle pushed through its weakened surface, burrowing inside the exposed opening.

Idly, Stringbean wondered what its intentions were. Did it want to carve a home from the supple wood and curl inside, soft and warm—or did it want only to feed, to chew the porch apart and leave once nothing remained? Her short fingernails picked at a scab on her knee while she thought, digging beneath her wound, the dried blood flaking to the surface of the porch, the new blood dripping down her leg to congeal on the bone of her ankle.

Her mind continued to fly, but it never landed, and Stringbean remained on the steps, the sun on the back of her neck, her face pressed to the wood, her mouth humming a song that would never exist again.

***

"Stringbean, come here," Widow Jahopson called from her chair in front of the window, where she sat and watched things Stringbean couldn't see. "It's time to cut your hair."

Stringbean padded over from the sitting room, running her fingers over the torn upholstery as she moved, her palm tracing the seam of Father Christoph's armchair, the tops of the sofa cushions, the splintered material of the wall. Habit. Everything in their house was a habit. Every day she woke up in her attic room, haphazardly covered her pallet with the blanket, and had a breakfast of vegetable shoots fried over the gas range. Every day Father Christoph led them in prayer, thanking Dog for such bounty, and then went out to the garden to compose a sermon. Every two weeks Widow Jahopson cut Stringbean's hair, so it lay ruffled and jagged on her head.

"Have you washed?" the Widow asked, wrapping a towel around Stringbean's neck. Stringbean nodded, delighting in the delicate pressure of Widow Jahopson's hands on her shoulders. The Widow was careful never to touch anyone, not even Father Christoph, so these bi-weekly allowances were a great pleasure to Stringbean, no matter how much she hated sitting still.

The click of scissors began to circle Stringbean's head chaotically, as Widow Jahopson slashed, wild, at any hair she could reach. Stringbean shifted often, uncomfortable in the wooden chair they borrowed from the kitchen, until the Widow stilled her with a firm hand. The afternoon sun came in through the window, catching on the scissors and sending wild beams of light onto the worn sofa, the radio, the carpet stained by Stringbean's many incidences of clumsiness and haste.

For a while they stayed quiet, in easy silence, until, so softly Stringbean almost didn't hear it, the Widow asked:

"How did you cut your lip?"

She had seen Bubba and his friends by the hill, and had fought viciously, but they had beaten her anyway.

"I fell off my bike."

The Widow sighed. "There were no bikes in the world Dog imagined, you know."

Stringbean forgave the attack on her bicycle, just as she would forgive anything the Widow did. She forgave the days of distance, and she forgave these haircuts, though they left her head looking sheared and ragged. The Widow's hair was long as a church window, beautiful flowing brown like the sky above the uranium mines. When she was younger, Stringbean had wanted to cradle the Widow's head in her hands, let her hair tangle around her fingers, but the Widow shied away from Stringbean as if she were coated in pesticide. It struck Stringbean that in the fourteen years since she had sprouted, she had never been held by the Widow, except that day almost four years ago when the mines had collapsed and killed six people. Even then the embrace had been brief and, Stringbean suspected, more for the Widow's sake then her own, an attempt to control fear by controlling someone else. The thought depressed Stringbean a little. Even Rose's father, though he worked deep into the night and most of the day, would kiss the top of his daughter's head when he emerged, before exchanging amicable nods with Stringbean and trudging off to sleep.

Of course, the Widow was not Stringbean's mother, any more than Father Christoph was her father.

On some untraceable instinct, Stringbean reached up to brush her hand against the Widow's. For a moment, Stringbean's calloused fingers touched hers, soft as a peach; then there was a violent jerk and the clatter of scissors falling to the floor, and Stringbean retracted her hand immediately.

"I'm sorry," she whispered, crestfallen. The Widow said nothing, but knelt silently and took the scissors into her hands. The *click click click* began again, blind as before.

This time the silence between them felt heavy as a heat wave. Stringbean tried to think of something that would make the Widow smile and forgive her, but nothing came to her mind except the numb loss of the Widow's hand.

***

"Things are very different from when I was your age," Widow Jahopson began, suddenly, her voice husky and low. "There was no drought, of course, and my sisters and I could drive to the ocean and swim. We went often... as much as we could. We always went together, and if we could not... we would not go."

"Did you live here?" Stringbean asked after a pause.

"No... no one lived here. I lived in the city with my sisters and mother. I had never even heard of Dog then, though of course he had already coaxed man from underground thousands of years ago. I drank water from a green plastic cup, and ate food from the grocery store. I swam in the ocean and my bathing suit was woven plastic, soft as milk." She sighed deeply, and the scissors stilled on the back of Stringbean's neck. The cold metal made her want to shiver, but she caught the instinct in the teeth so she could hear every word the Widow said.

"There are no cities now, little Peapod," she began again, the expression she wore impossible to guess from her controlled voice. "And while I know it is the will of Dog, I am sorry you will never see one. I'm sorry that... that you never had any siblings either. I loved my sisters; I was never lonely. You were never a lonely child, Stringbean, but... but I was always sorry you never had a brother or sister."

Stringbean thought of a little apple seed, dead in the back yard, but said nothing.

"Anne, my youngest sister, she died from toxin, and then Carla was crushed in an earthquake, and Liz ran off to the East and never came back, and Téa..." The Widow swallowed heavily, and resumed clicking her scissors. "I had to get out of the city. It was more wasteland than ever then. Whole blocks empty, with the lights flickering and the windows smashed... there was an earthquake almost every day, and the caverns had begun to open across the country. Ike and I packed up our car... I had driven the road we took many times—it was the way we took to get to the ocean—but I had never seen it so crowded before.

"I can hardly remember what it was like.... to see so many cars at the same time. Dog was with me, even if I didn't know it, and seeing all that metal on the highway... oh, it turned my stomach. I was not so delicate then, not so attuned to Dog, but this was enough to rouse me.

"Have you ever felt sick, Stringbean, when you the see the smoke above the plasticine factory? We had talked about me getting a job here, and Ike going to work in the mines, but we decided it'd be better to keep going. It did not seem safe... it was still so new and strange to us, a factory of that kind..."

Stringbean tried to think of a time before the plasticine factory had rested in the hills like a smoking crater. She had never thought about when it had been built— it had always been built. All the women who worked there, building little toys and stoves and (Stringbean shuddered) flowers— where had they lived before?

The Widow placed her fingers on Stringbean's temples, the scissors wrapped in her palm. "I felt a powerful thrumming, right here. Have you ever felt that, little one, when you say your prayers? This place, it needed me... something in me knew. I ran from our car; Ike ripped a chunk of my hair out trying to stop me... no, no, but I ran from him and from that car with all of our things pushed inside..." her voice was softer and softer, her hands shaking quietly against Stringbean's head. "And my body was so heavy..."

Everything in Stringbean wanted to reach out to her, but she kept her hands back, clutching her shirt at the hem.

Slowly, like the setting sun, the Widow withdrew. She unwrapped the towel from Stringbean's neck, and brushed rust-colored strands from her skinny shoulders.

"Go out and play, Stringbean," she said, her voice steady, as she pushed the fallen hair into a pile with the side of her foot. Stringbean stayed where she was, watching but not helping.

"How did you meet Father Christoph?" she asked, as the Widow moved into the kitchen to wash the scissors under hot water.

The tap ran for a few seconds, the whole house rattling with effort. Stringbean strained her ears and leaned forward, the chair back tipped onto two legs.

"Dog gives us one miracle," the Widow said. "And mine was that man."

Distantly, Stringbean heard the slash of scissors closing.

(PAUSE)

They skipped stones on the river. Stringbean showed Rose the wild, raging sections of Prominence: the waterfall, the bear cave, the chapel steeple; and Rose made each a place of contemplation, of curious, open study, moving from each stone or plant with wide, intelligent eyes.

"Look at this," she'd say, gesturing to Stringbean. "What do you suppose this is?" Like Stringbean, she did not wear goggles or a sun cloak, but Stringbean suspected it was for different reasons than Father Christoph's, and that Rose took the daylight as her due, and did not revel in the miracle of being.

But despite this, she was, Stringbean concluded, lying awake in her attic room and watching the shadows change, exactly what Father Christoph meant by the Grace of Dog: a person of peace and questioning, who saw beauty in all that He had planted.

When Stringbean haltingly tried to explain this, she was met by confusion in her friend, and felt embarrassed. She thought often, when she told Rose something, that there was a purposeful obstruction between them, as if their words could not reach each other. Where Rose was content to sit still, for hours even, pondering a question she had found along one of their journeys, Stringbean had no patience for anything but answers.

STRINGBEAN AND THE STORM

A strong wind had gathered; Prominence huddled together in the corridors of the grocery store and whispered what they heard, and what they heard was all the same: a storm was coming. A storm had crawled from the bristling stomach of the caverns, its mouth wide and eye wild, and now it charged on four legs to the seaboard, where it would finally be free.

Rain, said everyone without saying anything. *A storm.* Not the feeble centimeters of rainfall they received once every few months, not water excavated from the Earth or stolen from the river, but given, sent. Water they deserved! Water they had waited so long for, suffered so long for!

There was a fervor, quaking beneath a ceaseless calm. The congregation was insatiable, and Father Christoph shouted and shook and asked them all to shout too, for Dog was bringing water, for their prayers had been heard; Shout! Shout with all Dog gave you, for is this not proof that he is listening? The pews were sticky with sweat and froth when the service ended, and the air still echoed with celebration.

There were even rumors that the mines would close; the rains were expected to be so great that they'd flood the tunnels, but no official order was given.

Stringbean alone was untouched by the excitement. She based her expectations for the future on the events of the past, and how could she long for a storm when she had never even seen one? How could she fear earthquakes when she had never felt the ground beneath her feet collapse and disappear? And so she remained indifferent to the coming squall, ignoring the news reports and the blooming crop of umbrellas that burst from front porches and back doors, sudden as a tempest.

Truthfully, Stringbean did not fear much, but the thought of the sun disappearing behind black clouds frightened and confused her. She'd lay awake on her threadbare cot late into the night, turning the idea over and over in her head. Would she freeze, when the sun was held by the crashing rainclouds? Would Stringbean, who grew on the sun and loved it with the whole of her flat, flawed, soul, would she disappear when the sun did?

"It won't be gone," Rose told her, not smiling, though it was clear that she wanted to. "It's never gone. Even at night, it's just on the other side of the world." But this also confused Stringbean, and so she was not comforted.

***

"Ten!" Father Christoph said, his face toothy and ecstatic. "Ten inches of rain, they're saying! Can you believe it?"

Stringbean and Widow Jahopson exchanged a dry look, and then returned busily to their plates of fried vegetables. Who hadn't heard? Even alone in the forest, cramped in her secret tangle of weeds and branches, Stringbean could hear the whisper of rain. The animals were frantic for it—she heard their heavy, graceless footsteps stumbling through the underbrush, heard them murmur to each other, *"Ten inches, ten inches of rain!"*

The radio buzzed wild and alive. Father Christoph turned to it every few minutes and listened, his head cocked, as if waiting for a noose to fall. Stringbean smiled at his crooked posture, her mouth full of food, her sticky fingers resting lightly on a blue napkin that had been as permanent to her life as her legs or lungs.

"What will we do," the Widow wondered aloud, "with all that water?"

Father Christoph's head turned, and his face seemed free and open and far away. "What will we do?" he asked, surprised, and the radio squealed with static that made them all flinch.

***

The air had a different smell now: there was no smoke or dust in it, but something clean and fresh, like the smell of air-conditioning. The porch steps felt swollen beneath them, breathless and full.

"Have you ever been in a storm?" Stringbean asked, watching the sky. The sun was still heavy, no clouds in sight.

"A few times. Where I used to live." Rose puffed out her cheeks and brushed a sweaty lock of hair from her face. "It was strange. Like being splashed in the face when you're swimming. But not really like that. It's lighter, and warmer. And it smells good."

"It does?"

"Yeah. Really good."

Stringbean looked down at her expectantly, and Rose laughed, reaching her hand back to brush Stringbean's ankle. "I can't explain a smell! Can you?"

"Sure," Stringbean said, picking at a splinter lodged in the fat of her palm. "I can do anything."

"Oh yeah?" Rose challenged, twisting her body to face Stringbean, her smiling face shaded by the rungs of the porch. "Do it."

Stringbean was silent, thinking, for maybe the first time, of words; thinking, for the first time, of a sentence before she said it. It rattled her, this direct disregard for her instinct. She looked out across the yard, at the dry grass which ringed the yard in a tired circle; the twisted wooden fence, collapsed in places, sturdy in others; the peeling white paint of the porch railing beside her; and, over the tree line, the steeple of the chapel, a raised fist in the sharp blue sky.

"I," Stringbean said, her voice an exhausted triumph, "smell like the sun."

***

The rumors of rain were sounded from one home to another, whispered through screen doors, clattering over windowsills and cement stoops. Their children were forbidden to play outside, to wander too far from home and risk getting caught in the storm; even Bubba Vetch was threatened with imprisonment, though he was certainly no longer the boy who had so audaciously shorn his sun hood and goggles as a child; no, he had become tall and lean, big enough to know better, big enough to resist the temptations of a storm.

"We just don't know where it comes from!" his mother explained, wiping her thin mouth with a bright red napkin, its fabric a scar on the dining table. "So much water—what polluted places could that rain be made of?"

There is no pollution, Bubba remembered Father Christoph saying to him once, back when he had spent afternoons playing in the rectory's garden. *There is only what Dog made, and what we have done to it.*

"It's just water, ma," he mumbled, his hand toying nervously with his glass. It was a mistake to interrupt his mother from her fervor, but a strange and unwanted loyalty had settled on his shoulders with the heaviness of a wave.

Mrs. Vetch's eyes flashed. "It is not just water." Pale fingers stabbed at a plastic lily that had become imperceptibly uneven. "It is radiation, and poison, and disease."

Bubba felt a shiver, involuntary, at the mention of disease; sickness haunted his thoughts always, and, in the early hours of the morning, he would become convinced that the three years he had spent unprotected from the sun had jeopardized his remaining days. Mournfully, he chewed his food, remembering the itching pain of a sunburn and the color of the sky.

"Have you been taking your vitamins?" Mrs. Vetch asked, after she had tremulously swallowed her square of meatloaf.

"Yes, ma."

"And did you give Freddy what was coming to him?"

"Yes, ma."

"Show me your fists, John. Did you bruise them? Show me your fists." And her spindly hands unfurled across the table, groping for his.

"Ma, no, come on…" The thought of being touched by his mother's bloodless fingers turned Bubba's stomach, and again he thought of something Father Christoph had told him, in a whisper, so Stringbean could not hear.

"John, show me your fists."

"Ma."

"John!"

"For God's sake," his father said, spitting into his plate of food. "Leave Bubba alone. He doesn't need fists. He's perfect."

***

The wind was rising now: it pulled at people's clothes their hair, their faces. Excitement was rising too—it was alive. Rain, said the air. Rain, said the dry rasp of grass blades brushing against themselves.

Rain, said the gasping citizens of nowhere, their mouths open and their heads tilted back.

***

"Oh Dog, high in the kingdom of Heaven, send your people the water we long for! Have we not been good?" His face was red, sweaty, smiling; his face was like a face in a dream.

"We have been good!" they answered, whooping and cheering and turning to the windows to see if clouds had gathered.

"Have we not been gracious?" he demanded, pounding a fist on the pulpit.

"We have been gracious!" What a question! What had they not been grateful for, what had they not thanked Dog for in their lives, what did they have which they did not owe to him?

"Have we not been thirsty?" Father Christoph cried, throwing his head back, opening his arms as if already enveloped in the squall.

"We have been thirsty! We have been thirsty! We have been thirsty!" Oh, they rose like a tide, they stood and shrieked and moved with promise. The pews rattled and creaked in the frenzy and Father Christoph, Father Savior, roared and conducted as if his words parted tides, as if the rain came from his hands.

"Dog, would you hear the call of your people, would you hear the song we are sounding! Dog, give us this one miracle! One miracle!"

Miracle after miracle leapt from the pews, raising their voices as they begged for one more.

***

"Are you still nervous?" Rose asked, hushed. It was darker now. The sun was sinking like a boat full of holes, in a lake that was perfectly still. Stringbean almost couldn't see Rose, just the outline of her, the halo of her body. Her shoulder was close to Stringbean's hands, her white dress hanging loosely from the angle it made with her neck.

"No," Stringbean said, firm, running a finger along the porch railing. "It doesn't go away, it's just behind the clouds."

"That's right."

"When will it happen?"

"I don't know. They say today."

"Today's almost over."

Rose sighed a heavy, impatient sigh. "That's how it is."

Stringbean wanted to reach out, to say something comforting and kind, but that was not the way she had been made, and she could not see Rose anymore. There were many things she wanted, and being around Rose seemed to extend them, to bring them out from the other side of the world. She wanted to show her the treasures on her windowsill: the dented harmonica, the pale blue shard of sea glass, the dented can of soda pop that had grown faded and sticky from years of sitting in the sun. She wanted to tell her secrets, to bring her somewhere silent and say something she had never said out loud.

"I…" Stringbean stuttered, into the darkness. "I… I think…"

"It's okay," Rose said, and leaned back against String-bean's knees. She kicked the heels of her white sneakers against the bottom step as the stars began to appear, holes in the fabric of the sky. "It's a nice night."

Stringbean couldn't say anything, and kept her hands clasped firmly together.

"What are you thinking about?" Rose asked, turning away from the night. "You aren't usually so quiet."

"Nothing," Stringbean said, keeping words in her mouth like the sun on her skin, like the moment of weightlessness after you crash and before you land. Rose looked at her skeptically, her face shaded and fine in the darkness, but she did not say anything, and Stringbean was glad. Rose's shoulder blades dug into Stringbean's shins, and the porch creaked, and the town was quiet for a moment, the whispers finally silenced, even the crickets hushed. *That's how it is,* Stringbean thought, but the weight of someone else, the closeness and heat of another person, pushed her disappointment away.

It's a nice night, she smiled, brave and battered, her body alive with the energy of a lightning bolt, a clap of thunder that never came.

(PAUSE)

Father Christoph stretched his arms above his head, smiling in the fresh sunlight. The garden struggled with vegetables and vines and the bitter stalks of sweet peas, but Father Christoph did not despair. He knew the rain would come, one day or another. Warm and content, Father Christoph said a prayer to Dog, one of many he had said today. He had prayed when he awoke, prayed while he cooked breakfast, prayed when he left a little platter outside the Widow's bedroom door, prayed when Stringbean stumbled downstairs, her hair mussed and her eyes sleepy, prayed a little prayer of thanks when she chewed and swallowed without breaking anything. Sweat ran over his forehead, and he thanked Dog for that too.

Oh, Dog above, he thought, turning the dirt with his hands. *Thank you for this day. Thank you for the sun risings, and the leaf spreadings, and the flower bloomings. Thank you*, he smiled, as he heard Stringbean singing to herself while she washed the breakfast dishes, *for Stringbean. And thank you*, he winced, as he heard a plate shatter and Stringbean's muffled cursing, *for patience*.

STRINGBEAN AND THE LETTER

It was the shape of the words that stuck in Stringbean's throat, and how silently they twisted to form the sounds on the page. Even if she forced patience, keeping her movements slow, her brow furrowed, frustration began clouding her eyes, and her body began to shake for relief. One of her hands picked at the soft corners of the book cover, unconsciously; she would never purposefully damage one of Rose's belongings, which all carried a special weight in Stringbean's mind. This treasure, especially, was one Stringbean had always greatly admired: the book's face was a soft yellow, with raised black font that Stringbean, so tactile a creature, delighted in running her hands over, but by far the greatest feature was the cover-illustration. A little stuffed rabbit, its eyes sad and its fur frayed, peered out at Stringbean, the lines of its body heavy and determined against the yellow background.

Stringbean would quietly seek out the book whenever she was in Rose's home, poking through the stacks of abandoned and crumbled items until she found this particular thin, tattered volume. The rabbit's mournful stare and crooked posture reached something hidden in Stringbean, a girl who had never seen art or beauty, and she felt a shuddering emotion whenever she flipped through it, uncomprehending, but content. She liked the hardness of the pages, the smell of dry ink and wet paper that stuck to them, and the warmth the book seemed to carry, the remnant of many years of being loved.

Her obsession did not go unnoticed by Rose, but her friend was only amused by Stringbean's constant return to a book that she had outgrown many years ago and even her brother was growing too old for. It was not until yesterday, spurred, in part, by a particularly foul mood at something her father had said, that Rose had asked if Stringbean would want to borrow the little book, since she seemed to enjoy reading it so much.

Stringbean had nearly broken from shame, for of course she could not read, and Rose knew this well. Often, in times of kindness, Rose would read books aloud, ostensibly to practice her speaking, and Stringbean would sit beside her, trying to follow along with the words, but mostly just listening. Once Rose had written out the alphabet on a torn envelope and left it in Stringbean's room, for her to ponder fruitlessly many nights in a row. But the other girl, when in the throes of a temper, had no qualms at striking Stringbean where she was most vulnerable, attacks made all the worse by the knowledge that Stringbean could not retaliate. Her natural meanness, hot words and viperous scowls, had no effect on Rose, who could cripple Stringbean with one pointed question or sharpened smile.

And so Stringbean had slunk back to the rectory, her shame heavy on her shoulders, the book, a totem of her defeat, clutched in her arms.

Now, flat on her back in the living room, Stringbean struggled through its wrinkled pages, a trial almost uninterrupted since the day she had received it. Mouthing the words she recognized, sounding the letters she knew,

Stringbean tried to untangle the book's meaning, but her knowledge was too small, and the challenge too large. She closed her eyes periodically, keeping the book in front of her, and then opened them without warning, as if she could catch the sense of the page unaware, as if the words would suddenly fall into place. But, of course, they did not, and Stringbean jolted along, no closer to understanding than before.

Her frustration was beginning to peak, her hands becoming fists around the cover, when she heard the clang of the mailbox shutting, a dry sound that cut through Stringbean's toil. They did not often get mail out here in the rectory, and so the sound took a moment for her to place, a blessed moment away from the unfathomable symbols before her, a question that had an answer she could reach.

Mail was not very exciting to Stringbean: she liked to go to the post office, and she liked to lick envelopes, but the letters that were delivered to their mailbox were always for Father Christoph, and he never revealed their contents to her. She waited, the book resting open on her chest, for someone else in the rectory to call down that the letter was theirs, or else ask her to go and get it for them, but Father Christoph was in town today, visiting members of the congregation, and Widow Jahopson had spent the day in bed, demanding water and silence.

Stringbean was not helpful by nature, but her displeasure with the book was so great that any escape was preferable to its continued torture. She lifted herself from the carpet with a groan, stretching and flexing and setting her bones in order. The carpet was so thin and tattered that it was almost like lying on the bare floor, but Stringbean was not allowed to sit on the couch in her dirty clothes. The book she carried with her, out of nervousness, placing it down only to force open the front door, which had stuck to the doorframe in the hot day.

The mailbox leaned on the perimeter of the yard, its post imbedded in the dirt road outside the fence. Vaguely, as she walked, purposeful in the dry grass, happy to be free and feel sun, Stringbean remembered a time when the mailbox had been painted a pure sky blue, fresh as the white siding of the rectory. Now, both were faded and chipped, but so slowly had the paint fallen away that Stringbean had not even thought to notice, and would not have noticed now if she had not been so happy to be out of the house. Indoors were poison to Stringbean, who hated closed spaces and stale air; already the shame of reading had faded in the pleasure of being outside. The sun was spitting in the sky, heat so intense that Stringbean's lungs felt burned, and before checking the mailbox, she covered her hand with part of her t-shirt, so the metal tab would not sear her skin.

There was only one letter, resting innocuous and clean in the jaws of the box, and it was remarkable. Not for any physical reasons, for in that sense the letter was extremely ordinary: stark white, flat, a yellow stamp placed precisely in the corner. In fact, the letter had almost nothing distinguishing about it, nothing that would separate it from the hundreds of letters that had arrived at the rectory in the past sixteen years.

Except it was a letter, and it was addressed to Stringbean.

Her name, its length and shape, was familiar to her, like a bone. She had seen it written out many times, by Father Christoph, in his twisted, jointed writing, or by Rose, at some urging of Stringbean's, but to see it in the handwriting of someone she did not know made her heart pound and her head swim. How beautiful it seemed, rising from the tide of words and numbers she did not know, like an island or a mountain! That word was her, and she, she was Stringbean!

With shaking hands, Rose's book still safe under her arm, Stringbean peeled open the envelope, careful not to tear the paper. And there it was again, her name, right at the top of the page! She read it with mounting pride, reveling in its size, the anarchism of its shape, hard at the beginning before drifting into the softness of vowels and the leaning of an 'n'. An incredible joy washed over Stringbean as she ran a tentative finger over the length of her name: there she was, emperor of the page, and when she was gone the words would still be there, and if anyone wanted to know who she was they had only to find this envelope with her name inside.

The rest of the letter meant nothing to her, not even physically; neither the handwriting nor the scent of the paper were familiar. She wondered, for a moment, if this was some cruel prank of Rose's, a further embarrassment for Stringbean. But she had seen Rose's writing before, remembered its cramped, perfect spaces, and this letter did not have that precision. The words tilted into each other, became scrawl, and lifted again, like a boat bobbing in the water, culminating it one cresting signature at the bottom of the page.

Stringbean was frozen in the hot air, the letter clutched in her stone hands, her thoughts disjointed. The novelty of the letter created a distance between her and it; she could not grasp that someone, someone she did not know, had something to say to her, something she could not immediately recognize.

But then the understanding dawned, and Stringbean, wild and strong, was off. She moved without indecision, racing to the porch, placing Rose's book gingerly on the top step, and then careening towards the shed where her bike was kept, her long legs hardly touching the ground. The dirt road crunched beneath the tires, the frame rattled dangerously, but Stringbean could not slow her pace.

***

She arrived at the overpass heavy with sweat, her breath coming in dry heaves, but she did not pause. With an uncoordinated leap, her bike was pushed aside, and Stringbean was sprinting to Rose's door.

"Rose!" she cried, the letter clutched in her knocking fist. "Rose, I need you!"

The makeshift door opened partway, and Stringbean breathed for the first time since she had left the rectory. At last! At last, questions which had buzzed in Stringbean's mind for so many years would be answered!

"What do you want?" a reedy, whining voice asked, and Stringbean felt her stomach fall as if from a great height, dashed against rocks, for it was not Rose who stood in the doorway, but Gabe Jr., a sickly scowl on his face.

"Is your sister here?" Stringbean asked hopelessly: she could see the whole of the house through the doorway, and it was clear the pale, weak boy was alone.

"She's out with Dad," Gabe Jr. sniffed, pulling on the door so its hinges squeaked. It was a nervous movement, not one intended to annoy, but it riled Stringbean anyway. "What did you want?" His voice was like Rose's, but where it imparted strength and opinion in his sister, Gabe Jr. sounded perpetually hurried, as if the world was moving too slowly around him.

Stringbean felt a shiver of shame. To admit her shame to anyone, especially someone smaller and weaker than her, would be death to Stringbean, but the letter, and more importantly, its answers, outweighed the shell of pride ensconcing her.

"Can you…" she began haltingly, not meeting the eyes of the diminutive boy before her. "Do you know how to read?"

Gabe Jr.'s brow furrowed in disbelief. "Can you not?"

A spear struck Stringbean, threatening to double her over with pain; the picture before her swam, and her eyes closed on reflex. *Is there any escape from humiliation? Will no one forgive you, Stringbean, for what you cannot control? Does it matter to anyone that it wasn't your fault?*

"Why didn't you learn how to read?" Gabe Jr. demanded, his eyes alive with curiosity, just like his father, his sister.

"I didn't want to," Stringbean mumbled, and it was true. She hadn't wanted to go to school, and she had not been forced to. Father Christoph insisted that Dog would give Stringbean any knowledge she needed, as long as she prayed and was kept watered and warm. It was unclear what the Widow thought, or if she even cared that Stringbean was wild and feral.

"When will Rose be back?" she asked, a desperate question. It was clear that Gabe Jr. would be no help to her; he was too young, adored Rose too greatly, and resented Stringbean for taking his sister's attentions. No, Stringbean could not afford to expose any more weakness to him, not if the letter contained what she suspected it did.

Gabe Jr., his face still cruelly disbelieving, shrugged. "I don't know. My dad's looking for something, and she's helping."

Stringbean felt the letter in her hand, crumpled as she was. Gabe Jr.'s mean eyes, black like Rose's but without the spark that illuminated hers, cut deep into Stringbean. But what, she thought angrily, would Gabe Jr. know about wanting, with a father and a sister and love—strange, conditional love, but love all the same? What would Gabe Jr know about letters?

"Don't tell Rose I came by," she said miserably, too dejected to instill the command with any venom. As she pedaled away from the underpass, she knew that he would not listen to her, but she did not know how Rose would react, and she did not want to think about it.

★★★

With growing agitation, Stringbean paced the worn living room, her hands running along the furniture with each circuit: sofa, armchair, radio, end table, over and over and over. The carpet was spongy, like moss; the wood, where the carpet ended, a foot from the wall, creaked under her weight. She did not touch the Widow's rocking chair, it was sacred. She did not look out that window, though it afforded a better view of the yard, but instead craned her neck out the adjacent one each time she passed, and watched the road, the sun, and the mailbox. Then, when it was clear that no one was coming, she paced again, not allowing her eyes to focus on anything.

The day had been endless. She had biked home, reclaimed Rose's book from the porch, but could not stand the thought of reading when the letter was so nearby, so inscrutable. What had been left to do? She couldn't go outside, for fear Father Christoph would arrive while she was gone. She couldn't wait upstairs; what if she fell asleep from pure anxiousness? So she paced, and paced, and with every finished circuit the day came closer to passing.

The sun was already low and fat when she saw his form appear at the end of the road, a long, dark shadow splayed out in front of him, his gait calm, almost mocking Stringbean's desperation. Confronted with his sudden appearance, her body was seized by nervousness, and she felt like she would collapse, or suffocate, or cry. But she could not wait any longer, and out the front door she charged, leaping off the porch steps, reaching him just as he passed the fence into their front yard.

"Father Christoph! Father Christoph!"

His weathered face smiled. Here was Stringbean, coming out to meet him after an interminable day! Her hair was sticking up, and her tattered red T-shirt was too big for her wiry body, but she, as always, carried with her an incredible grace, a sense that she was truly comfortable in her surroundings. He was struck, suddenly, by how tall she had become, and struggled a moment to recall how old she was, and how old he was, and how long his life had been shared with this strange, kinetic creature.

"Hello, Peapod!" he called jubilantly, and he wished he could reach out to ruffle her hair. "How was your day?"

But the day, the day of frustration and shame and waiting, would not allow Stringbean to answer that question. "Read this!" she pleaded, pressing the envelope, sweaty and creased from the journey, into his hands. "Please, please, Father Christoph, read it."

With infuriating slowness, he unfolded the letter, shifting his body so he was in the fading sunlight. "Why Stringbean," he exclaimed, with confusion, "this is addressed to you!"

Stringbean could hardly stand in his ignorance, and her rage was like an object, falling from the sky and killing them both. Would there be no relief from this day of exclusion; would anything be easy? She wished that she was alone, down by the river skipping rocks, throwing stones at birds, anything physical and simple that could erase the pain of today.

Father Christoph's face had grown still, pale and vivid; his eyebrows were furrowed. He did not look like the man Stringbean had grown up with, who had brought her to life and taught her to pray; no, with his face so cold and blank, he looked like a stranger.

"What's it say?" Stringbean asked, suddenly afraid.

"Nothing," he laughed in answer, and his voice was both hot and cold. "It's just a regular letter. It's nothing important."

Stringbean felt as if she had been hit across the head.

Her ears were ringing, her vision was ringing. "Father Christoph," she started, reaching out to him, to pull his sleeve, pull herself back into the world. His eyes had become unfocused, scanning the letter over and over. He seemed to have grown taller: his face was mask-like, and though he was not shouting, the air felt like he was. She had seen him angry, on the pulpit, but this was not anger, and it frightened her. She tried to remember ever feeling afraid around him, and to remember what she felt when she was with him usually.

"Father—"

"Enough," he growled, and then Stringbean's letter was just paper, torn strips of paper, fluttering in the hot air like snow. "Now, I never want to hear anything about this again. It wasn't important, and there's no reason to talk about it. Do you promise me, Stringbean? Do you promise to forget about this?"

"I promise," she repeated, alarmed, terrified, confused. "I promise." She did not know how many times he wanted her to say it; his body was shaking, his mouth a hard white line, his breathing controlled.

"Come inside, Stringbean," he commanded, but the words had no weight, and he did not seem to notice he was saying them. "Come inside; it's time for dinner."

But Stringbean could not look at him, and, after a slick silence, he left her behind. The air felt empty, as if something had been torn from it, as if it had been burned. Stringbean knelt to the ground, bowing to where her letter once was. She tried to find the scrap of paper that held her name, rooting through the dusty fragments until her eyes began to water, but it must have been ripped in half, and, incomplete, she could not recognize it.

(PAUSE)

What is there in this world for you, Stringbean, once your youth has dried up? What else can you do, when you can no longer run and climb and eat the sun that hangs low from low-hanging branches? Will you work in the plasticine factory? Die in the mines? What is there for a girl like you, wild, unconquerable Stringbean?

"I want to be an astronaut," she answered, with childish sullenness.

"You can't," said Rose, dark head bent over her math problems. "You can't count."

Stringbean's smudged features fell easily into a frown. "How high do I have to count?" she demanded, her arms crossed, her plans shaking.

Rose paused in her work, forcing her voice to stay level, to expose no laughter. "Oh," she said, with forced carelessness, "at least to a hundred."

This stopped Stringbean cold. Twenty, maybe, but a hundred? It could not be done.

"I want to be a mailman," she said after a silence, and Rose could not hold back her laughter now: it spun pure and perfect over the porch steps, and anyone who heard it would have laughed too.

"You can't," she said, smiling, eyes wet. "You have to stay here with me."

STRINGBEAN AND THE WHALE

What's your record, Stringbean? How many skips can you get in a row? "Eight, usually," she answers with surly pride. "But one time I got one to land clear on the other shore. That's about twenty skips." If there was one thing Stringbean was built for, with her long arms and jutting hips, it was skipping rocks. Watch her wind up: the coil of her bones, the retraction of her hand, deft with purpose, and then, like the flourish of a letter, the release, *flit-flit-flit*, eight skips, ten skips, twenty skips to the opposite shore. Would you like to do the same, Stringbean? Fling yourself across the river and emerge, dizzy, on the other side?

"No," she says, taking careful, blind steps as she searches the shore for stones. "I'm fine the way I am."

And she was—Stringbean was fine on this shore, her sleeves rolled up, her bike against the sea wall, her ankles lapped by the gentle river waves. The sun was warm on her neck, and the water was cool, and with each curl of her body, the stone clutched behind her head, she could see Rose, the barest flicker before Stringbean hurtled through space, but that was all Stringbean needed, and at times, all she could take.

"How many was that?" Rose asked, when Stringbean's

form finally faltered, a little stutter of breath that relaxed her wire muscles.

"The last one?" Stringbean clarified, turning her head so she could see Rose in full, sitting on the sea wall with her dark hair curling in the sticky heat. Stringbean looked down again, pretending to think. "About seven." A shrug, still not looking up, as if she were in church. "Not so great."

"Not so bad either," Rose said, but without interest, and she was lost in thought again. Her cheek rested against one fist, and her visage was stormy. Stringbean remembered, with a shiver of embarrassment, the day she and Rose had met, and how she had wanted to push the dark expression from the smaller girl's face. Now, knowing how permanent the shadow was to be on her friend's countenance, she wondered how she had ever wanted to destroy it.

Not, Stringbean conceded, *that I like her better this way.* For while Rose's furious inward expression delighted Stringbean in a kind of vicarious way (she never sank so deeply into her thoughts, or had thoughts deep enough to sink in), there was a danger that came whenever Rose was pondering a particularly difficult question, usually one her father had given her: the danger that she might sink so far she would not return. Sometimes Rose's eyes would glaze over, and Stringbean would tug gently at her hands until she came back with a confused smile. For a moment, Stringbean feared that this was one of these spells, and she studied Rose with a new urgency, but then Rose sighed in frustration, and crossed her legs, and Stringbean's heart relaxed.

"Stringbean," Rose called, her tone cross, but no less distracted than before. "Come up here please." As quickly as Stringbean's heart had breathed a little huff of relief now it felt tense and trapped, as if any sound it made would send some rabid pursuer on its trail. She stumbled up the rock shore, her feet catching on sharp stones that she, in some strange, sudden blindness, did not see until they were biting at her unprotected soles.

Rose probably wanted to ask her a question; she enjoyed exposing how little Stringbean knew, especially when she herself felt unsure the answer to a difficult puzzle. Just the other day she had embarrassed Stringbean by asking her to read a notice outside the post office, a shame so sharp and total that Stringbean had slunk off to the rectory and gone to bed right after supper.

But Rose didn't seem to be in that vindictive sort of mood today; when Stringbean sat down beside her, reaching out nervously to play with the white material of her companion's sundress, Rose did not smack her hand away. Instead, she turned to fix Stringbean with a serious expression. "Listen," she began, but then drifted again, and seemed to forget where she was altogether. Stringbean listened. She listened to the hum of the air around her, to the lazy march of the river, to the clattering, disorganized thoughts alive in Rose's head. She listened to her own heartbeat, erratic, and felt, from a distance, that same kind of love she had carried as a child, a sureness of self, being, and Dog.

"Rose?" she asked quietly, pulling at the hem curled between her fingers. "Rose, come back."

And awareness began to enter Rose's features, but they did not focus on Stringbean, rather, a point behind her, somewhere in the river.

"What is that?" she said, and it was a question for them both, not for her to wonder to herself, or for Stringbean to suffer vainly over. Stringbean turned her head and saw what seemed to be a log, floating up the river, but the sight of it made her stomach clench, as if she might throw up. There was something wrong about the object, the black form maybe twice as big as Stringbean, something perverted and strange. The river seemed to shake, the air seemed harsh. Wordlessly, the two of them hurried to the shore, but it was Stringbean who waded into the water with strong, sure steps, and Rose who remained on the edges, watching her progress without saying a word.

***

The current was weak, tugging limply at Stringbean's t-shirt before giving up and moving along. It was cool on Stringbean's skin, a relief from the harsh sun and the exertion of the day. She pushed the water aside, her movements deft and focused. She had always been a strong swimmer, and it felt natural to return to the river, to tread the channel as she had so many times before, even if now there was an urgency throbbing beneath her tongue.

The creature was drifting closer, rising placid and huge from the water. Stringbean, immediately, was reminded of a missile, or a bullet, the creature's body tapering from a spherical head into a slender tail. *Like a comet,* Stringbean thought, an immense comet floating across an inky black sky. For a moment, the being did not seem as evil as before, as if it had always belonged in the river, but then its stench smacked Stringbean with the force of a wave. The smell was crippling, like bones in the sun, like gasoline. Stringbean could taste it in her mouth, and her eyes began to water, her throat to clench and suffocate.

With a start, like missing a step, she remembered a day with Bubba Vetch, as children, when she had become caught in a current and was dragged beneath the water. The feeling of drowning was so vivid that she was surprised that she had forgotten, had not thought about it in years. She wondered if there were other things she could not remember, other places she passed every day that held a part of herself she had forgotten. She was almost to the center to the river, just an arm's length away.

Up close, the creature was a terror. Its blue-gray skin was scarred, tumorous, and seemed to pulse with pain. One of its flippers had been shredded, so it trailed graceful and free in the water. Even the soft curve of its shape and wide face could not assuage the horror Stringbean felt, could not block out the low keening noise it pushed between its wedge of a mouth. Stringbean did not let herself feel fear, or shy away from the animal's suffering. With her final reserve of strength, she reached out and, with her fingertips, turned the mottled creature towards the shore.

When it was perpendicular with the riverbank, she shoved her shoulder beneath the creature's intact fin, straining with effort. Her feet slipped uselessly along the silt, and she swallowed a mouthful of water in one misstep, surfaced choking and sputtering. But it was not far. Nothing was as far as it had seemed when she was a child. She was halfway there already, halfway back to where Rose stood, unmoving, her white dress like a scar on the black beach.

With delicate steps, when Stringbean had collapsed in the shallows, the creature resting mute and heavy beside her, Rose crossed the remainder of shore to where they lay. Stringbean, out of breath and shaking, tilted her head in surprise. Rose hated to get her feet wet. She hated all physical discomforts, especially cold.

"What is it?" Stringbean huffed, red faced. Rose kneeled beside the poor creature, pushing her dress up from the water, so Stringbean could see a breathless stretch of thigh. Her expression was guarded, but not the natural sullenness of Rose's temper; it was guarded because she did not want Stringbean to see what she was thinking.

"It's dying, Stringbean," she said in a voice that meant nothing. "Do you know what death is?"

Of course she did—had Stringbean not felt death's claw marks every day she lived, warnings in sermons, prayers before bed? Had she not killed as well, pouring cans of soda down anthills, throwing stones at the heavy, thirsty birds on the rectory fence? Had she not wished death on others, when she was in a particularly foul mood, when she felt hurt or wronged in some way—on those occasions the whole world could die: Father Christoph, the Widow, even Rose.

"When I was ten a part of the uranium mine fell in and killed six people," she said instead, and Rose nodded, but did not respond. It was not, Stringbean realized with a sinking feeling, the answer she'd been looking for.

The creature breathed a strangled breath, and the girls looked at each other, alarmed. "What do we do?" Stringbean asked. The creature began to moan horribly, its immense bulb of a head shaking with agony, and she could not hear Rose's response over its yowling, its gentle eyes squeezed shut. All she could see now was the black maw of its mouth, the hard bone walls of its teeth, the chasm of its body. From a great distance she heard Rose shouting, but she couldn't make out what she was saying. Her breath wouldn't come. The smell was horrible.

What do I do? she thought. She felt no fear. She had, it seemed, been waiting her whole life to confront the blackness of the creature's mouth, its stomach—darker, she was sure, than space, any space that Dog lived in. She would return to the darkness she had come from, buried inside Dog's creation, unable to breathe air or feel light or see the sizzling blue of the sky. A bead of sweat traced the inside of her knee. Again the creature screamed, a wall of sound that knocked Stringbean further into the water. *There's nothing I can do,* she thought, and from behind her eyes came an incredible question, without words.

When she blinked, the thing was dead. Its labored breathing had ceased. Its eyes were empty. In a rush, her lungs filled with air, and suddenly she was heaving, the stench of death caking her entire body. Rose's arms descended on her, stroking her hair and holding her shivering form close, saying things Stringbean could not hear.

"It's just a little thing, Stringbean, just a little thing that's died, that's all…"

***

They let the current take the body away. Stringbean could not look at the shore and sat facing the forest, the train tracks, the chapel spire, far away like a stray mark on a drawing. Rose watched the slow-moving water, and sighed when the creature's remains were added back into the river, drifting lazily to wherever the water was going.

"Stringbean," Rose said, more gentle than Stringbean had ever heard before. She wondered what she looked like right now, to make Rose sound this way. "Stringbean, I have to tell you something."

Stringbean saw that it was important, from the creases in Rose's face, but she could not bear to focus on the real world just yet. She let the words flow past her, watching the way Rose's mouth shaped each syllable.

"Are you listening to me, Stringbean?"

Blushing, Stringbean shook her head.

Rose frowned. "Why are you like this?" she asked, taking Stringbean's chin in her hands, examining her split lip and bruised eye. She sighed, before letting go and leaning her head on Stringbean's shoulder. "I wish we could take you with us when we leave."

Stringbean felt her body go cold. "Leave?" she asked, her mouth like cotton.

Rose nodded, not seeming to notice how still Stringbean had become. Stringbean was always moving, tapping her feet or playing with her hands. "We're going East." Rose's expression grew stony. "To the caverns."

"You can't," Stringbean said, trying to sound sure and

brave, but her voice shook anyway. How could Rose leave? Her Rose, stumbling through the lightless passages of evil beneath the earth? Her Rose, in the clutches of Cannibals and beasts and crushing darkness? Rose's laugh buried deep beneath the earth, her puzzled frown locked away forever? What was Stringbean's life without her thoughtful, direct presence, without her always on the outskirts of her vision, the edge of her mind?

For a moment, it looked as if Rose was angry, her mouth hard and pinched, but like a stone slipping from the shore, her face grew soft. "We have to," she said, wrapping her hand around Stringbean's. "You know how it is."

Did she? Stringbean was not sure she did. The current was drifting away again, the corpse disappeared. Where had it gone? Was that something else Stringbean was supposed to know?

Far away, too far for Stringbean's mind to wander, the body of the last whale turned in dead pirouettes, unrushed by the silty water. Its fins splayed haphazardly, its eyes saw nothing. It was peaceful, almost: a totally free object, slipping farther and farther away from Stringbean like a stone she had flung, *flit-flit-flit,* crashing through the dark water, never feeling the sun again.

(PAUSE)

In a past life, or another life, Stringbean, with her low-slung gait and piercing frown, must have been a dog. Not often, but sometimes, their mannerisms intersected, and the animal swagger of a Boxer sank into her legs, the stoic posture of muscle, and there! that characteristic snarl! Oh yes, Stringbean had been a Boxer; one, it is to be sure, that lived loudly and died bravely, just like Stringbean herself.

STRINGBEAN AND THE MIRACLE

The cracks were beginning to show. Something had cracked in Prominence—there was a thirst in the air, a broken hunger that would never be sated. It was not noticeable, what had changed: the plasticine factory still churned sour smoke on the cliff's edge, the mines still hummed beneath the surface of the town, the chapel was still alive and loud on Sundays and Wednesday afternoons. But even so, something had changed: something had been lost, or taken, or finally broken, and Prominence had cracked on the edges.

Stringbean too, was tired. She sat hunched on the dusty porch, a hand shading her face, and watched the slow drift of clouds above the chapel. The churchyard seemed to have a sepia stillness, a quiet, gentle picture moved only by the light breeze and the tolling of the church bell. The congregation stood in relaxed groups, shaking hands and laughing and nodding their heads. Even the bright clothes of church-going, the rich pinks and whites and soft yellows of dresses and button-up shirts, seemed muted to Stringbean on such a dusty day.

She smiled at a knot of children kicking the dirt into red plumes, jumping and chasing and weaving in and out of their parents' clutches. Small thoughts played in Stringbean's mind, her own wild dominion over the children she had known, whose names and faces she could not bring forward. She had scrapped with all of them, had risen to any challenge and excised those who could not rise to hers. She remembered playing in the sun, pretending to be a king, or a knight, or a solider with a gun. She remembered Bubba, and his stumbling attempts to follow her wherever she went, real or imaginary. What were the children of the congregation playing, she wondered; were they warriors or astronauts?

But a change seemed to have struck the children. Where once they were rough and scampered without direction or intention, now a small cluster had gathered beside the wooden fence on the edge of the clearing, and while they still ran crazily through the crowded churchyard, they had a center, and to it they always returned.

Stringbean sat for a moment, her chin in her hands, pondering this shift. But she had never been a contemplative person, someone who could figure without the facts before her, and though she dreaded entering the fray of the congregation, she stood, stretched her long limbs, and headed to the corner of the yard.

The crowds, not as great as when she was a child, parted for Stringbean, as they always had. Her bare feet crunched in the dirt, and often it seemed that some unsuspecting person would crush them beneath their heel, but no one came near. Their hands did not brush against her tanned skin; their eyes did not travel her gaunt face. Stringbean, for her part, moved carefully, and did not breathe until she had reached the edge of the clearing, and only the crowd of children and the toxic blue sky stretched before her.

It was a tribute to the children's distraction that they did not notice Stringbean approach. Stringbean, because she was big, and because she was forbidden, appealed to children immensely. They loved to watch her from a distance, huddled together on the edge of the yard, while she completed her chores or just sat, staring. It would seem that they were undetected, and would titter and grow bold, when suddenly Stringbean would turn with a ferocious face that sent them screaming and laughing back to parents.

"What's going on over here?" she asked. Her voice sounded strange to her, cracked and old.

With a squeal of fear and delight, the more cowardly children fled in dizzying circles, tripping over themselves and each other in their haste to get away from the terrible, cannibal Stringbean. They too, did not touch her, though it seemed sure that one or two would, so chaotically did they flee. But they knew not to, and then it was just Stringbean, her strange, wide eyes staring down two girls, who stared right back without fear.

"Go away!" one of them cried, the older one, though only by perhaps a year. Her arms were outspread, blocking Stringbean's view of the far field.

"This is our thing!" the younger girl spat, and Stringbean was shocked at the rage seizing her tiny body, the furor that shook her sweet blue eyes and dirty blond curls. She had a strong forehead and a protruding lower lip that she had twisted into a scowl; an identical expression rested on the other girl, and Stringbean realized with a start that they must be sisters.

For a moment the two of them were united in an unshakeable tantrum, and Stringbean, though she was big and strong and brave as a general, felt a creeping wariness in her stomach. She was reminded of Bubba, and how unstoppable she had felt with a companion behind her. But then another gust of wind blew, and the smaller of the girls stumbled in its grip, and Stringbean shook the feeling away. They were children, no matter how fearsome their faces were, and Stringbean was a child no longer. Bending at the waist, she wrapped a wiry arm around each girl's middle, and, despite their protesting words and fists, lifted them over her shoulders. Their howls were violent, and they tore at Stringbean's hair, but she did not let them go until the rungs of the fence were a thin blur behind them.

"We're telling our Mom!" the older sister shouted when Stringbean deposited her burden on the other side of the churchyard. Their faces were red with tears, either from embarrassment or frustration, and as they ran to the woman Stringbean assumed to be their mother, she felt a pang in her stomach. She would get in trouble for this later, when word reached Father Christoph of what she had done, but Stringbean was always in trouble, in one way or another.

***

When she returned to the fence, passing ghostlike through the thronging congregation, Stringbean scanned the field for what the girls had been focusing on. At first there was nothing but dry heather and emaciated trees, the landscape that had owned Stringbean her whole life; her brow furrowed, and the beginnings of a question entered her battered head. Had it been a pretend game, one that she had grossly misinterpreted from her excluded position on the porch? Had it only been a play, one she had not understood, and not been invited to understand? But then a flurry of movement at her feet caught her eye, and she crept beneath the lowest rung of the fence, her body not making a sound.

Writhing in the dry grass, not even an arm's length away, was a thick, black snake, the kind that hid beneath log piles or basked on the flat stones of the river. Stringbean had never seen one so close before, and its dark glow, its wrathful eyes, the delicate pink of its open mouth, held her in breathless awe. With fevered desperation the snake lifted and struck and tangled in the grass, but it did not seem to be caught in any way, though its actions were suffocated with the desire for escape.

If Stringbean were younger, she would have lifted a stone from the dirt and struck the serpent down. There was no doubt in her mind that, had Stringbean been a child, the snake would be dead at this moment, his corpse a trophy for her windowsill. She would not have missed; she would not have been afraid. But Stringbean did not reach for a weapon. With uncharacteristic calm, she leaned against the rotted fence, and watched as the snake continued its strange ritual, its leaping, twisting dance.

Only when the church bell tolled the end of another hour did the snake cease its seizure and slip into the wilderness. Its black body was like a slicing blade, a poison in solid form, and watching it disappear with the fluidity only a killer can affect, Stringbean felt a throb in her stomach, a sudden stabbing pain.

***

She did not get sick, Stringbean; no, she was strong, like an animal. She had never been sick a day in her life. She had never suffered through the sympathy of others, wailing from beneath her bed sheets while wraiths filled her lungs with hot water and sponged her forehead. Stringbean was not afraid of the world the way we are: she did not balk at filth or cold weather, she never buttoned her coat.

So the shiver in her stomach, the shiver of pain, did not occur to worry Stringbean. It just swirled in her body, and she did not notice. She was not unfamiliar with pain— riding her bike, climbing trees, picking fights, Stringbean had a pull for bruises and cuts. But the pain that slithered through her bones was not what she thought, no, not what it seemed.

"You seem down, Peapod," Father Christoph remarked at supper. Stringbean's plate was still full, and steam had stopped rising from the food. "Are you not hungry?"

"I am," Stringbean answered, surprised. She had not noticed anything strange about her behavior, though now, thinking about it, she could not recall a time when she hadn't wanted to eat. Without a word, Widow Jahopson took Stringbean's plate and divided the cold vegetables between Father Christoph and herself. Stringbean felt a strangled panic, but she could not understand why. "I'm fine. You don't have to do that," she said, reaching for her plate, but the Widow dismissed her, not looking up from the table.

"Go to bed, Stringbean," Widow Jahopson said, when she had finished chewing. "Don't forget to say your prayers."

"It's only seven," Stringbean protested, but without any anger. It didn't seem worth it, and that too surprised her—when had she not felt a hot breath of rage at any injustice, any assertion that she was a child? But the energy did not come to her, and, without another word, she left the table and stumbled up to her bedroom.

She did not pray to Dog to wake her, or deliver orders, or carry her soul to Him should she lose it in the night. She had not prayed in years, though she could not remember when she had stopped. Before Rose left, but after she arrived, of that Stringbean was certain, but to think hard about that window of time pained Stringbean, and so she did not try. It didn't matter anyway. Dog had never had much to say to Stringbean.

***

An animal whined in the middle of the night, and Stringbean felt the light of awareness, struggling on the edges of a shadow.

"What is that?" she mumbled into her dream, but nobody was there to answer.

Someone could have come for Stringbean. Father Christoph could have come in through the back door, his hands covered in dirt, holding her in his arms like the day he found her, so long ago in the creeping weeds of his vegetable garden. Widow Jahopson could have dragged herself, pale and weak, up the stairs, to act on what she had sworn so long ago. Or Bubba, poor Bubba, who Stringbean missed with a dull ache every day, could have crossed the porch with his raised fists and been brave for the first time.

Or Rose, wherever she was, far away from Stringbean. Why was no one there when Stringbean needed them?

No, Stringbean, little shiver, would not be saved.

That isn't an animal, her head begged. *Stringbean, wake up, wake up: that's you.*

And it was; that inhuman moan, echoing wet and desperate, was the unbreakable Stringbean. The pain in her stomach was a fire crackling, coils of flame chewing at her blood, her walls, her bile and her bones. It was worse than anything she had ever felt—worse than the day Rose had left, worse than being held beneath the water, worse than the day her seed had died and her heart had nearly burst.

Stringbean's jaw was locked, and no scream slipped through, only the pathetic whining that had woken her. Spit was pooling in the lines of her face, overflowing and running down her neck. Her muscles had seized, wound tight as if someone was holding her down, covering her mouth so she could not make a sound. To scream! Oh, to shriek like she had when she was a child, gallant and fearless. Stringbean wanted nothing more than to scream, and then, when the world knew what it had done, to die.

This wasn't the way Stringbean deserved to die, too broken to call out for anyone who wanted to hear. Die on the shore of the river, in the arms of someone who cares.

Die in the grip of space, hurtling to the unknown. Die beneath the earth, looking for something you'll never find. Don't die like this, brave Stringbean: covered in spit and sweat and resignation. Don't die like this, strong String-bean: your body shaking and your eyes in your head and no words in your throat.

Scream, little miracle: live another hour.

And with a *crack* like a bone breaking, her mouth opened and Stringbean screamed. She screamed for help. She screamed for release. She screamed for everything she had done, and everything she hadn't. She screamed for everyone who she had loved, big as the grace of Dog, loved with every beat of her mean, mean heart. She screamed for herself, even if she didn't know who that was, screamed for the girl from a seed and a prayer and a mother and a father.

It shook the house, her scream, and Father Christoph started awake and thought of a broken man on the train tracks, begging for a sign. His old body tore up the stairs, its weakness forgotten, and he thought of a little girl carrying a watering can, her arms shaking with effort. He knelt on the floor, the grace of his life in his arms, and thought of all the miracles he had received, and begged for one more.

It shook the Widow from her stupor, the scream of her heart and the sobbing of the man who had saved her, saved them both. Pain, Widow Jahopson knew pain, and when she rushed to Stringbean's side she knew it again, held it to her chest and breathed it in. How could a life be so much pain? How many families would be torn from her? How would she bear living anymore, if this wild girl, writhing in agony and screaming like a fire, was not living beside her? Without Stringbean, laughing with the Father on the porch, wandering through the living room with her fingers running along the couch and the chair and the walls, where would the Widow be? She didn't know, didn't care, and pressed her hands to Stringbean's stomach and did what she had done her whole life: she prayed, and she closed her eyes, and she begged the pain away.

It shook the world, Stringbean's scream, and the world held its breath and covered its ears, but she did not go away. She did not grow weaker, and she did not grow quiet, and she did not flicker into nothingness. She was alive. She was alive and had been her whole life. She had been hated, and pained, and left behind, but she had always lived. She had been strong, and brave, and mean, and bad. She had been loved. She shook in Father Christoph's arms, she sobbed beneath the Widow's desperate hands, and she knew that she had been loved.

It's a miracle, she thought, cried, when something inside her burst, and the pain was so great it didn't seem to be there at all. A miracle to have been born into this dying world, to have felt the sun's daggers on her skin, to taste food that would soon be gone. A miracle to have told Bubba stories, and held Rose's hand, and sung songs in the garden with her delicate make-believe friends. A miracle to have been Stringbean, just Stringbean, and lived as beautifully and perfectly as she had, a little girl in a world of her own, a little seed, big as the sky.

It's a miracle, she thought for hours, feeling Father Christoph unwrap his arms, feeling the Widow push her hair back and close her eyes. *It's a miracle to have gotten here.*

And, quietly, her long face relaxed, her fingers curled and gentle, Stringbean thought about where she had come from, and how far it was from here.

STRINGBEAN AND THE GRACE OF DOG

Where are you going, Peapod? Your home is that way. Turn around, poor little Stringbean—it's not too late. Go back to Father Christoph, listening to the radio while he works in the garden, notes for a sermon sketched onto his palms, laughing at jokes only he understands. Go back to Widow Jahopson, sighing in the mirror, humming while she walks, wiping grime from your face with the side of her thumb and a wistful smile. Go back to your porch, your riverbank, your secret clearing and attic room, go back for the treasures you've found, you've stolen, you've been given. Oh, Stringbean. It's too late now.

She didn't think while she crossed the overpass, her step easy and untroubled, her eyes clear and focused. How long before things became unfamiliar? Here was where Rose used to live. Here was where she and Bubba used to hunt bugs. Here was where Stringbean rode her bike, two hands, one hand, no hands. Follow this road to the plasticine factory, vomiting smog even while calamity raged. Turn here to go to the grocery store, where, Bubba had promised her, every food imaginable was laid out to feast upon. Keep walking and who knows where you'll end up, your feet torn and your throat dry, begging to belong.

Where else can I go? Stringbean wondered, but she didn't let herself find an answer. She didn't want to think about the rectory, its walls sagging and roof untiled, the dirt path to the mail box, the wooden fence keeping the forest at bay: the only place she could always return to. Where else could she go?

The road was sparse now, the trees disappearing, and, surprised, Stringbean noticed the sun was rising. She didn't feel tired. She didn't feel anything, not even the ache in her body that had settled the day she had broken into Mrs. Vetch's soul, the day she knew she was not who she had thought.

What had I thought? Her bare feet crunched on dirt, no road anymore. A little seed, a giant prayer, the breath of Dog. What had she been thinking? But that didn't matter anymore; she had believed what she believed, and that was just fine.

The trees were all gone now. Even the dirt was fading, mixing into coarse, grey stone. *The caverns*, Stringbean concluded without emotion, pausing to take in its expanse, its infinity. There was nothing out there: Stringbean could see forever, and all she saw was nothing.

What's left to do, Peapod? Are you sure there is nothing you have forgotten?

Little Stringbean, brave and weak and strong and afraid, rolled up her sleeves, pushed back her hair, and breathed. Tall, lanky Stringbean, heart thrumming in her slight chest, narrow shoulders squared, walked into the Earth, walked away from the world she was born in, walked away from the moment of grace she had been beginning.

Oh, Dog, she thought, as the walls grew darker, *keep them safe. Keep them the best you can.*

Oh, Dog in heaven, keeper of us all, there goes your girl, just the way you made her.

About the Author

Geneva Zane received her BA in creative writing from Bard College in 2018, where she received the Lockwood Prize in Creative Writing. Her novel, *Stringbean and the Grace of Dog,* was a finalist in the 2018 Fence Modern Prize in Prose: Literature Appropriate for Children. She has been published in *PCC Inscape, The Perch, Chronogram* and *Hanging Loose* magazine. She lives in the Hudson Valley, by the river.

OTHER TITLES AVAILABLE FROM
Pink Narcissus Press

SUSPENDED HEART
Stories by Heather Fowler
"It's a dazzling collection of magical realism, from boys made of clay and girls made of razor blades, to Philip Dick-esque replicants, to vampires and heroic parrots." —Jen Michalski, author of *Close Encounters*
ISBN: 978-1-939056-15-3

DAUGHTERS OF ICARUS
New Feminist Science Fiction and Fantasy
"Throughout, the authors explore themes of gender, identity, and autonomy, with characters as diverse as miniature clones, stripper vampires, aggressive mermaids, and mystical crones. Many of the stories focus on gender roles and the pull of relationships, whether parental, familial, or romantic, among all kinds of people." —*Library Journal*
ISBN: 978-1-939056-00-9

THE BIRTHDAY PROBLEM
A sci-fi novel by Caren Gussoff
"Gussoff packs a punch in this multi-layered and beautiful narrative. Strange and wonderful, *The Birthday Problem* presents a Pacific Northwest fractured and transformed, but always well worth the visit." — Cat Rambo, author of *Near + Far*
ISBN: 978-1-939056-06-1

www.ingramcontent.com/pod-product-compliance
Lightning Source LLC
Chambersburg PA
CBHW060233180626
46813CB00007B/3065